THE SCARLET LETTERS

CW01497435

Ellery Queen was both a famous fictional detective and the pen name of two cousins born in Brooklyn in 1905. Created by Manfred B. Lee and Frederic Dannay as an entry in a mystery-writing contest, Ellery Queen is regarded by many as the definitive American whodunit celebrity. When their first novel, *The Roman Hat Mystery* (1929), became an immediate success, the cousins gave up their business careers and took to writing dozens of novels, hundreds of radio scripts and countless short stories about the gentleman detective and writer who shared an apartment on West 87th Street with his father, Inspector Queen of the NYPD. Dannay was said to have largely produced detailed outlines of the plots, clues and characters while Lee did most of the writing. As the success of Ellery Queen grew, the character's legacy continued through radio, television and film. In 1941, the cousins founded *Ellery Queen's Mystery Magazine*. Edited by Queen for more than forty years, the periodical is still considered one of the most influential crime fiction magazines in American history. Additionally, Queen edited a number of collections and anthologies, and his critical writings are the major works on the detective short story. Under their collective pseudonym, the cousins were given several Edgar awards by the Mystery Writers of America, including the 1960 Grand Master Award. Their novels are examples of the classic 'fair play' whodunit mystery of the Golden Age, where plot is always paramount. Manfred B. Lee, born Manford Lepofsky, died in 1971. Frederic Dannay, born Daniel Nathan, died in 1982.

THE SCARLET LETTERS

ELLERY QUEEN

THE LANGTAIL PRESS
LONDON

This edition published 2013 by
The Langtail Press

www.langtailpress.com

ISBN 978-17-80-02166-9

It is ordered that Miss Batcheller for her
adultery shall be branded with the letter A.

—UNKNOWN, *Records of Maine Province* (1651)

It was around this law that Nathaniel Hawthorne wove
the story of *The Scarlet Letter.*

Contents

A ...

Until the fourth year of their marriage, their friends considered Dirk and Martha Lawrence one of the happiest couples in New York.

The lovebirds were invariably described as "nice, interesting young people." The temporal part of the description puzzled outsiders at first, since both were in their thirties, not the prime youth of the biologists. Besides, Martha was two years older than Dirk. But after people got to know them the description came easily. Dirk was cast in the dark, romantic mold of Bohemian garrets, and Martha had the plump, exquisite look of the pigeon aperch on the sill. That they were interesting and nice was never questioned at all. Dirk was a writer, and to non-writers–who comprised most of the Lawrences' friends–writers are curiosities from another world, like movie stars and ax-murderers. And Martha was an absolute darling–that is, she was no threat to the other women in their set.

Still, those who esteemed the Lawrences as interesting and nice would have been astonished, had they ever thought of going back over the statistics, at the amount of evidence to the contrary. There were times, especially in the third year, when Dirk was far from nice–when he lost his temper publicly at nothing visible to the human eye, or when he had had two or three Scotch old-fashioneds too many. And even a writer can become a bore when he makes a scene or gets nastily drunk. There were times when Martha was a very dull pigeon indeed; these were usually the times when Dirk was being far from nice. But no one thought of these dabs of episode as being related to a large canvas. Their only effect was to make the Lawrences seem as human as other people at a time when they were in considerable danger of being dropped for their inhuman felicity.

Ellery got to know the Lawrences through Nikki Porter. He had seen Dirk Lawrence now and then at meetings of the Mystery Writers of America, in the days when Dirk was turning out his dark, unpopular mystery novels, but they had not become friendly until Dirk married Martha Gordon. Martha and Nikki had known each other in Kansas City; when Martha came to New York to live, the two girls met again, liked what they rediscovered, and became inseparable.

Martha Gordon had come to New York not to seek her fortune but to live on it. Her mother had failed to survive Martha's birth and her father, a meat packer, had died during the war while Martha was touring the Pacific with a USO troupe–she had worked hard in dramatics at Oberlin and she was with a Little Theater group when the war broke out. Mr. Gordon had left her a great many millions of dollars.

Ellery found Martha an intelligent, sensitive girl unspoiled by her money but lonely because of it.

"When they tell me how gorgeous I am," Martha said grimly during a bull session in the Queen apartment one night, "I point to the plank. And they all tell me."

"You're oversuspicious," Ellery said. "You're a darned pretty girl."

"*Et tu,* Ellery? Do you know how old I'm getting to be?"

"Don't bother looking around for a plank *here*," said Nikki calmly. "This one runs, Martha. I know."

"And there you are," said Ellery. "You ought to take Nikki with you on your dates, Martha. Her judgment of men is uncanny."

"Anyway," said Martha, "who wants to get married? I'm going to be a Broadway star or die in the attempt."

Martha was wrong on both counts. She failed to become a Broadway star, and she survived to meet Dirk Lawrence.

By this time Martha had worked out a technique. She lived modestly and her acquaintances were all people of moderate means. When Dirk Lawrence asked her to marry him she was working in the office of a theatrical producer at a salary of sixty dollars a week. He did not learn that his bride was a millionaire until they set up housekeeping in a third-floor walkup in the East 30s.

Ellery knew the Lawrences as well as he knew any of Nikki's friends, yet he never achieved a solid feeling about their future. The trouble, he suspected, lay not so much in Dirk's thin royalties and Martha's fat dividend checks as in Dirk's psychological economy. Dirk acted as if he had been invented by Emily Bronte—fierce, brooding, a little uncouth, and strange in sudden ways.

But it was this very quality in Dirk's nature that attracted Martha. To the little blonde wife, her big swarthy scowling husband was an uncredited genius, a great and tragic figure. The truth was, they were drawn to each other because of their oppositeness. Dirk was always preoccupied with his problems, fancied as well as real; there was not a self-centered bone in Martha's sturdy little body. He demanded, she fulfilled. He sulked, she diverted. He stormed, she soothed. He doubted, she reassured. She satisfied completely his evident needs for a worshipful ear, a bosom to lay his head on, and a pair of soft maternal arms. And Martha was happy to provide the ear, the bosom, and the arms.

It should have been a sound enough basis for a marriage, but apparently it was not. Toward the end of the third year, when the change became noticeable, they seemed unable to stay in one place.

It was usually Martha who started the running. But Ellery had noticed—on the evenings when he and Nikki did the town with the Lawrences, or went to a party, or engaged in any activity which involved mingling with other people—that Martha's flights were a sort of conditioned reflex, arising out of Dirk's threat to settle into one of his moods. Dirk's dark mouth had a trick of turning up very slightly at one corner when he was about to sulk or get angry; the appearance was of a smile, but the effect was unpleasant. At such times, whatever Martha was doing or saying was dropped immediately. She would jump up and say, "I feel like a bowl of vegetables and sour cream at Lindy's," or whatever—Ellery felt—happened to pop into her mind at the moment. Then Dirk would pull himself out of it, and off they would go, hauling people along who could see no reason for not staying where they were.

Occasionally, however, Martha's back was turned when Dirk's mouth pulled its telltale trick. Then he would either explode with terrifying violence over some trifle or begin to drink like a camel. Those were the occasions when Martha would suddenly develop a sinus headache and have to go right home.

In the fourth year their troubles came to a head. They were seen together less and less. Dirk drank steadily.

That was the year Martha found her place in the theater. She bought a play and produced it with her own money. There were parties which Dirk did not attend. At other times he would show up at rehearsal, or accost Martha in a restaurant, and make a scene. Martha burrowed into production details, seeing no one they had known, not even Nikki. When the play failed, Martha stuck out her little jaw and began to look around for another script. What went on in their home—by this time they had taken a plush apartment on Beekman Place—was no secret to their neighbors. There were quarrels early and late, sounds of breaking furniture, wild sobs and wilder roars.

Their marriage had collapsed. And no one seemed to know why.

Nikki was as baffled as the rest of their crowd.

"I have no idea what's wrong," she said, at Ellery's question.

"But Nikki, you're her best friend."

"Even your best friend won't tell you," Nikki said unhappily. "Of course, it's Dirk's fault. If only he'd stop making like Edgar Allan Poe!"

Then, one beautiful night in the early spring, Ellery and Nikki learned what was wrong with the Lawrences.

It began with a Western Union messenger. He leaned on the Queen buzzer just as Nikki was tucking Ellery's typewriter into its shroud for the day.

"It's addressed to you, handwritten," Nikki said, coming into the study with an envelope. "And if that's not Martha Lawrence's handwriting, I'm a monkey's aunt. Why should she be writing to *you?*"

"You sound like a wife," Ellery said, jiggling the cocktail shaker. The day's dictation had not gone well and he was in no mood to be nice to anyone, especially the lone witness of his frequent exhibitions of anguish. "All right, Nikki, hand it over."

"Don't you want me to read it to you while you make the cocktails? After all, what's a secretary for?"

"The cocktails are made. *Give me that!*"

"I don't understand," said Nikki without rancor as Ellery tore open the envelope. "Something awful must be happening. Of course, if you'd rather I left the room ..."

But the note made them both grave.

4

ELLERY DEAR—

I've tried everything I know, which apparently isn't enough. This can't go on. I need help.

I'll be on a bench in Central Park, on the main walk approaching the Mall from the 5th Ave. entrance at 72nd St., at around 9:30 tonight. If by some horrible coincidence you should see Dirk or hear from him between now and then, *don't for God's sake breathe one word about my having asked you to meet me.* He thinks I'm seeing Amy Howell at the Barbizon about a play-script.

I'll wait till 10. *Please come.*

MARTHA

Nikki was staring at the notepaper, with its uneven scrawl. "Holy matrimony," she said. She deliberately kicked Ellery's desk and went over to the couch and sat down. "It's past working hours, so you can act like a gentleman—if that's possible of any man. I want a drink and a cigarette … Poor Mar. This marriage was going to last a thousand years, like Hitler's Reich. You're going to meet her, aren't you?"

"I don't know."

"You don't *know?*"

"If it was a case, Nikki, of Dirk's stealing something or murdering somebody—"

"How do you know it isn't?" demanded Nikki fiercely.

"My dear child—"

"And don't 'my dear child' me, Ellery Queen!"

"—this is chronic. It's been going on for over a year. It's simply a case of two people who started out for paradise on a raft finding the damn thing sinking under their bottoms four miles out. It happens every day. What can I do for Martha? Hold her hand? Take Dirk into St. Pat's by the seat of the pants and read him a fatherly sermon to a playback of the Wedding March?" Ellery shook his head. "The middleman in a situation like this is sure to get it in the neck."

"Are you through driveling?"

"I'm not driveling. It's just that instinct tells me to stay out of this."

5

"I ask you only one question," Nikki said, rising so suddenly that part of her cocktail slopped over onto her last pair of nylons. "Are you going to meet Martha tonight, or aren't you?"

"But it's not fair," protested Ellery. "She ought to go to a clergyman. I mean I haven't made up my mind."

"Well, I have. I'm through."

"You're what?"

"Through. I'm throwing up your pitiful little job. Get somebody else to finish your book. It's no good, anyway."

"Nikki!" He caught her at the door. "Of course, you're right. It reeks. And I'll go."

"Oh, it's not so bad, Ellery," said Nikki softly. "There are some parts I think are positively brilliant ..."

Ellery found Martha on a park bench in a deep shadow. He very nearly missed her, because she was all in black, including a veil. It was as if she had deliberately dressed to blend with the night.

She caught his hands as he sat down.

"Martha, you're shaking." Ellery felt that levity might help. "Isn't that the approved opening line?"

He was wrong. Martha began to cry. She snatched her hands away and put them to her face and cried into them in a deep, dry, horrible way.

Ellery was appalled. He looked around quickly to see if anyone was watching. But the bushes behind their bench were silent and most of the people on the other benches ignored them. Tears in Central Park were no novelty to nature lovers.

"Martha, I'm sorry. I really am. Won't you tell me what's the matter? It can't be as bad as all that. Things seldom are ..." He went on in this dismal vein for some time. But Martha only cried more deeply, more dryly, and more horribly.

Ellery began to wish himself elsewhere. A few nearby heads had turned with indignation, then curiosity. And a large figure in a peaked cap, swinging a nightstick, had stopped strolling to stare at them very hard.

"Something wrong, bud?" boomed the large figure.

"No, no, officer," Ellery called loudly enough for their bench neighbors to hear, too. "We're just rehearsing a scene from our new play." He pulled his hat brim lower.

6

"Yeah?" The park patrolman lumbered over quickly as heads turned everywhere within range. "When do you open? I'm sort of a confirmed theatergoer myself. Me and the wife see every show I can rustle some ducats for—"

"Next month. Broadhurst. Simply mention my name at the box office. Now if you'll excuse us—"

"Yes, *sir*. But what name?"

"Alfred Lunt," said Ellery.

"Yessir!" The patrolman stepped back respectfully. Then he said to Martha, "Good night, Miss Fontanne," saluted, and marched off whistling.

Ellery said in a hurry, "Now, Martha—"

"I'll be all right in a minute, Ellery. This is so stupid of me. I hadn't the slightest intention of … It just happened …" Martha buried her face in his chest.

"Of course," said Ellery, looking around uncomfortably. Everyone was watching the rehearsal. "You've kept this in a long time. Naturally. Now just pull yourself together, honey, and we'll have a long talk." Ellery's left arm began to ache; Martha was jamming it against the slats. To relieve the ache he worked his arm free and draped it along the top of the bench. It touched Martha's shoulders.

"Lovers' quarrel?" said a voice.

Martha quivered.

Ellery turned.

Dirk Lawrence stood behind the bench.

Dirk's hat was plastered to one side of his head and his dark features had the fixed but pendulous set of the very drunk. The reek of whisky surrounded him. The eyes under their thick black overhang were unpleasant-looking pits.

"Hello, Dirk," said Ellery heartily. "Where'd you come from?"

"Hell," grinned Dirk. "And I'm looking for company."

Ellery found himself on his feet. But Martha was already between him and her husband.

"Go home, Dirk," she said in a shrill voice. "Please go home."

"Hell of a home. See what I mean?"

"Now look here, Dirk," said Ellery resentfully. "If that crack about lovers wasn't a gag, you're a bigger damn fool than I am. This is the first

7

time I've seen Martha in months. She wanted to talk something over with me—"

"In the language of the eyes, no doubt," said Dirk Lawrence dreamily. "My little Martha. My little nymph. You know something, Brother Q? You kid me not."

"Martha," said Ellery, "you'd better go."

"Yes, Martha my love, you do that," said Dirk. "On account of I'm going to teach this dirty feist to keep his paws off another man's wife—"

"Dirk, no!" screamed Martha.

Dirk stepped into a moonbeam. Ellery saw that some bubbles of foam had gathered in the twist of his mouth. His eyes seemed sober and sad. He backhanded Martha's face across the bench and she disappeared.

Involuntarily, Ellery stooped to look for her.

He never reached his knees. A bomb tore his head off and the back of it went *bong!* against the cement walk, followed by the rest of him.

The last thing he remembered was an outburst from the nearby benches as of many firecrackers.

It was applause.

"So now you know," Martha was saying. "Better than I could have told you, Ellery. I tried my best to keep him from following me. But I guess I'm not very good at it, and he doesn't believe anything I say, anyway."

"Have some more coffee, darling," crooned Nikki.

Ellery wished that Nikki would show some appreciation of his performance. His jaw had a green and purple lump on it and the back of his head felt as if it had bounced around in a cement mixer.

He had come to in the park to find his head in Martha's lap and a crowd of admiring spectators encircling them. Dirk was gone. The theater-loving patrolman was remarking with heat that he'd sure as hell like to run that hambone in for getting so carried away by his part—if Mr. Lunt would tell him the scene-stealing slob's name, that is—and by the way, here he'd been under the impression that Mr. Lunt was getting gray, or was that one of them there now hair falsies? In the end, hiding his face with his hat, Ellery cajoled the patrolman into putting them in a cab at the 72nd Street entrance, the only address he could think to give

8

in the mushy condition of his brain being that of the Queen apartment. And there was Nikki, who was supposed to have had a date with an obscure but paid-up member of the Authors League, waiting for his return. Martha had fallen into her arms, and the two women had disappeared in Inspector Queen's bathroom for a half-hour, leaving Ellery to administer his own first aid. Not even his father was home to cluck over him.

"But what's the matter with Dirk?" Nikki demanded. "Is he off his rocker?"

"I don't know," Martha said in the same draggy way. "I don't know what's happened to him. I don't think he knows himself."

"I felt no particular uncertainty," said Ellery, trying to move his jaw sidewise.

"You're lucky to be alive."

"Oh, come," said Ellery. "The brute punches hard, but not that hard."

"That's why I was so afraid," Martha said to her coffee cup. "I was afraid he had a gun with him. He'd threatened to start carrying one."

"Nikki threatens to quit every hour on the hour, Martha, but she's still affiliated with the firm."

"You don't believe me. I suppose I couldn't expect you to. I tell you if Dirk had had a gun with him tonight, he'd have killed you."

"And he'd have had a darned good case, too," Ellery said. "See here, I don't want to seem unfeeling, but give the devil his due. Look at it from Dirk's viewpoint—"

"Suppose you look at it from Dirk's viewpoint," said Nikki coldly.

"You told him a pretty feeble story, Martha, about meeting some female play scrivener at a woman's hotel. So he followed you. He saw you enter the park, pick out a nice dark bench. I came along, obviously by prearrangement. I sat down and the first thing Dirk knew you were cuddling against my manly breast and I had my arm around you. Your tears made it look even worse—as if you and I'd been having ourselves a thing, but I'd found a new chick to play around with and wanted out, and you were trying to hold on to me. What else could he have thought? After all, the man's only flesh and blood."

Martha shut her eyes.

"Like you?" said Nikki horridly. "Wives like Martha exist only in Victorian novels, and a husband who doesn't know it ought to be altered."

"Will you stop interrupting? Besides, Martha, Dirk was tight. Probably if he'd been sober–"

Martha opened her eyes. "When he's sober it's worse."

"Worse? How do you mean?"

"When he's sober, I can't keep telling myself that he's saying those horrible things because he's drunk."

"You mean Dirk actually believes you're sleeping around?"

"He tries not to. But it's become an obsession, something he can't control."

"May I say nuts?" inquired Nikki.

"Nikki, you aren't in love with him. I am."

"If he were my husband, I'd give him something to have an obsession about!"

"He's sick …"

"This is going to hurt," said Ellery. "Either he's sick, Martha–or he's right."

Nikki leaped. "Martha, I'm taking you over to my place this minute. This *minute.*"

"Sit down, Nikki, and shut up. Or go into the next room. If Martha wants my help, I've got to know what the problem is. I'm not going to deliver a sermon–I've seen worse crimes than adultery. So first, Martha, tell me: Are you what Dirk called you tonight–a nymph?"

"If I am, he hasn't caught me at it yet." Martha's face continued to show nothing. "Look, boys and girls, I'm a gal who's trying to save her marriage. If I weren't, I shouldn't be here."

"*Touché,*" said Ellery. "Now tell me everything you know about Dirk that might explain this jealousy complex of his."

About Dirk's childhood Martha was largely in the dark. He also had been an only child. The Lawrences were East Shore Marylanders, Southern sympathizers during the Civil War. Dirk's mother's family were South Carolina Fairleighs, with a distinguished history of slaveholding and aristocratic poverty.

Whatever Dirk had lacked as a boy, it was not material. The Lawrence wealth was inherited from his Great-grandfather Lawrence, who had gone West after Appomattox, made millions in mines and railroads, and returned to Maryland to restock the family coffers.

"Dirk's father never did a lick of work in his life," Martha said. "And neither did Dirk till he put on a uniform. His father sent him to VMI, but he was kicked out after a year for chronic insubordination. He decided he wanted to be a writer. Pearl Harbor caught him living in Greenwich Village, wearing a beard and trying to make like a poor man's Hemingway on an allowance of a mere ten thousand a year. He enlisted–in relief, I think– and he was an officer with the paratroopers in Belgium when he got the news that his parents had both been killed in an automobile accident.

"It wasn't till he got home after the war that Dirk learned two things: One, that the police suspected Mr. Lawrence of having deliberately run the car, with himself and Mrs. Lawrence in it, off the road–"

"Why?" asked Ellery.

"I don't know, unless it had something to do with the other thing Dirk found out when he got back. His father had run through every penny of the Lawrence fortune and had left nothing but debts.

"Dirk went back to New York, broke except for what he had on his back. He tried writing again, but after a few months of starvation he looked for a job. A publishing house took him on in the editorial department, and he was with the firm over two years. The job lasted till 1948, when he was twenty-eight years old.

"I've met some of the people he worked with there," said Martha, "and they all paint the same picture. Dirk was skinny and intellectual-looking–from not getting enough to eat–and he'd developed a black Russian attitude towards life. His long suit was irony, and of course he's brilliant. But he didn't get along with the other people in the office, women especially."

"Any particular reason?" asked Ellery.

"It might be this: Shortly after he landed the job, he began going out with a girl in the office. All I know about her is that her name was Gwladys, which she spelled with a *w*. She fell head over heels in love with him, they had an affair, and she soon became a nuisance. They quarreled and he stopped seeing her. And then she committed suicide. Of course, she was a hopeless neurotic, and it wasn't Dirk's fault, but from that time on he had nothing to do with women."

Dirk's editorial job had required him to read a great many mystery stories. They stirred his imagination, so he began to write again, this time attempting a detective novel. To his surprise, his own firm accepted it for publication. It sold just under four thousand copies, but the notices were good.

"That was the one he called *Dead Is My Love*," Martha said. "Ellery, what did you really think of it?"

"For the work of a new hand, it was surprising. The plotting was amateurish in spots, and the story had a wry quality, but it was different. I questioned Dirk about the morbidity of his writing when I first met him at a meeting of the Mystery Writers of America. His only comment was that murder is a morbid subject. That's when he quit his job and devoted all his time to the typewriter, isn't it?"

"Yes," said Martha. "He turned out three more detective stories in the next twelve months."

"I remember," Ellery nodded, "that Dirk would open up to me in that period when at MWA gatherings he'd utter hardly a word to anyone else. He was hurt at the small sales of his books while what he felt to be inferior products earned two and three times as much. He covered up by being defiant. When I suggested a brighter, less Gothic, approach, some compromise with popular taste, Dirk replied that that was the kind of stuff he wanted to write, and if people didn't like if they didn't have to buy his books. I thought at the time it wasn't a very grown-up reaction. I wasn't surprised when he stopped writing detective stories."

"That was my doing, I'm afraid," Martha said with a slight tightness. "You know, I chased Dirk. I decided to marry him three days after we met."

"You never told me that," said Nikki accusingly.

"There's lots I've never told you, Nikki. I used to write him daily mash-notes. I was perfectly shameless about it. I was the one who encouraged him, after we were married, to try a serious novel.

"And maybe that was my big mistake," Martha said. "He was so happy, he worked so hard. And when the book came out and got an even smaller sale than his detective stories, and most of the critics panned it brutally ..."

"*The Sound of Silence* was a bad book, Martha," said Ellery gently. "Souped-up realism that only succeeded in being slick melodrama."

Martha was silent. Then she said: "We had a time of it for a few weeks, but I finally loved some self-confidence back into him and he started on the next novel. And that turned out even worse …

"After the second book there wasn't a thing I could do to snap Dirk out of his depression. The harder I tried, the more I seemed to irritate him. When he went to work on his third novel, he locked himself in the study. And that was when I suppose I made my second mistake. Instead of hammering the lock off and pounding some sense into his thick head, I … well, I looked around for something to do. That's when I produced *All Around the Mulberry Bush*. The flop it took taught me a lot, and I knew I'd found the spot in the theater I'd been groping for before I met Dirk.

"I also thought," continued Martha in that dreadful calm, "that my fiasco would bring Dirk and me together again, on the theory of the sociability of misery. It only seemed to shove us farther apart. He accused me of going the route of all rich dilettantes, and we had a really bang-up row. I suppose I was terribly hurt for the second time … Anyway, back he went to his typewriter to sulk, and I bought my second play. And that's when this jealousy business showed up."

"Exactly how," asked Ellery, "did Dirk first manifest it?"

"You've met Alex Conn. It was my second production and Alex's first. There's never been an author more respectful of his producer. Poor Alex wouldn't dream of making love to me; he'd sooner try to embrace the Sphinx. Besides, he has a broad streak of lavender.

"Alex's play had to be rewritten before we went into rehearsal. I had definite ideas about how I wanted certain scenes to run, and I got into the habit of dropping into the hotel where Alex was working, a dirty flytrap off Times Square. Alex works best in his undershirt, with his shoes off, and one night Dirk burst in on us and, to my absolute amazement—and Alex's—accused us of having an affair. We thought he was joking. But the beating he gave poor Alex in that horrible hotel room was no joke …

"Nothing Alex or I said to assure Dirk he was imagining things had the least effect. He was—he looked—well, you saw him tonight, Ellery. Only that night he wasn't tight."

"I hope you told him off!" said Nikki.

"Well, I told him I wasn't going to act as if I'd committed a crime, because I hadn't, and I said a lot of other things, too, about mutual trust and faith and love, and the result was we wound up with our arms around each other and what seemed like the dawn of a new understanding. But the very next week, when I was talking over the role of Michael in Alex's play with Rory Burke, who eventually played it, Dirk made another scene—and that one got into the columns. And that's the way it's been ever since, and I don't know why, why, *why!*"

And suddenly everything gave way and Martha was sobbing. "If Dirk doesn't stop ... I can't take it much longer! He needs help, Ellery. I need help. Is there anything you can see to do? Anything?"

Ellery took her hand. "I'll try. I'll try, Martha."

Ellery put Martha Lawrence into a cab—she insisted on going home alone—and he went back upstairs to find Nikki filling the coffeepot from the kitchen tap viciously.

They had their coffee like two strangers in a cafeteria.

But then Nikki put her cup down with a bang. "I know I'll hate myself in the morning, but I've got to sit up and beg." After a moment, Nikki said, "Ellery. I'm begging."

"For what?"

"Oh, don't be obtuse! What can you do?"

"How should I know? You know the idiot as well as I do. Better."

Nikki frowned. "Personally, I think Martha's the idiot. But then, as she said, I'm not in love with him. Mar's done a lot for me, Ellery—things I've never told you and probably never will. And I not only love her, I like her. There's something so awfully *clean* about Martha. Like a little girl in a starched pinny ..."

"Maybe that's it. She's the last woman in the world, I should think, whom anyone would accuse of sleeping around. Especially her husband! That's why I'm so worried, Ellery. It isn't natural. There's something wrong with Dirk."

"Of course there is."

"And I'm scared."

"With reason." Ellery fingered his jaw unhappily. "But what can I do? It's a doctor Dirk needs, not a detective."

14

"Doctors don't know everything."

"They know more about this sort of thing than I."

"He's committing a crime!"

"So is the soda jerk who doesn't wash the glasses properly, but I'm not expected to solve that kind of mystery. Nikki, I'd like to help, but it's not my kind of problem."

"It might turn into your kind of problem!"

"All I can do is see Dirk tomorrow and try to help him help himself. Although, after tonight, I don't think I'm qualified to do even that! ... Nikki, would you see if there's any codeine in the medicine chest?"

But it was Dirk who came to see Ellery.

He showed up at the Queen apartment just as Inspector Queen was sitting down to breakfast.

"Ellery?" The Inspector eyed Dirk suspiciously. "He's still in bed, Mr. Lawrence. Someone hung one on his chin last night, and he was up half the night feeling sorry for himself. You wouldn't know anything about it, would you?"

"I hung it," said Dirk Lawrence.

The Inspector stared at him. Dirk needed a shave, his clothes were damp and wrinkled, and his dark strong face was lumpy with fatigue. "Well, you don't look very dangerous this morning. Through that door and to your left."

Dirk said, "Thank you," and went through Ellery's study to the bedroom beyond. Ellery was lying on his stomach, nuzzling an icebag.

Dirk lowered his big body into a chair beside the bed and he said, "Don't be alarmed. My intentions this morning are strictly to crawl on my belly."

"This is a dream," said Ellery in a muffled voice. "At least I hope it is. It would mean I'm getting some sleep for a change. What do you want?"

"To apologize."

"Good. Get me some coffee, will you?"

Dirk raised himself and went out. He came back with the coffeepot and two cups and saucers. He poured for both of them, lit Ellery's cigaret, and sat down again.

"I wouldn't say," remarked Ellery, looking him over, "that you passed a restful night, either."

"I walked the streets."

"All night? In the rain?"

Dirk looked down at himself with some surprise. "Say, it rained, at that."

"Then you haven't been home?"

"No."

"Haven't you even phoned Martha?"

"She wouldn't talk to me if I did."

"You underestimate Martha's capacity for being kicked in the rear. That woman is too good for you, Lawrence."

"I know," said Dirk humbly. "She has the patience of a setting hen. I realize now she only met you to talk about me. But that's this morning. Last night I was plotzed."

"I have it on the best authority," said Ellery, sipping his coffee, "that you do pretty well when you're not plotzed, too."

Dirk did not answer at once. His dark skin was gray under the stubble and his eyes looked trapped. He leaned back and shut them, as Martha had done the night before.

"Have you ever had a real set-to with yourself, Ellery?" His voice was a faraway rumble.

"Yes."

"And lost it?"

"Yes."

"And kept losing it?"

"No," said Ellery.

"Well, that's the spot I'm in. I can't explain this in rational terms, and yet I'm not irrational ... at least I don't feel I'm deluded ... It sneaks in. I can't keep it from sneaking in, Ellery. And once it's there I can't seem to dislodge it. It sticks, no matter how hard I try. I see Martha with another man, and I feel myself blowing. Am I making any sense?"

"Not much," said Ellery, "but then sense isn't the word. Call it non-sense, and I get it. What *reason* have you for continually questioning Martha's fidelity? Because there must be a reason."

"I always think there's a reason—at the moment. This thing generates its own reasons."

"What thing? Let's name names."

"This jealousy ... phobia."

"Too simple, Dirk. Call it a cuckold phobia, and you've got something. I don't mean to pry, but what's the matter with your sex life?"

Dirk's eyes flew open, and Ellery blinked in their flash. But then the flash died, and the big man sank back in the chair again.

"That hurt?" inquired Ellery

Dirk passed his hand over his face in a curious lavatory gesture. "Look," he said. "I'm sorry for smacking you last night. Let's leave it at that."

He got up.

"Down," said Ellery. "Down, Dirk. I'm not finished with you. I happen to like your wife, and you're giving her a rough time. This thing has to have some roots. Let's dig ... Thank you," he said, when Dirk suddenly sat down again. "I pumped Martha last night, and between what I got out of her and what I've gathered from personal observation, I think what's wrong with you, Dirk–and it's not restricted to this jealousy business by any means! – goes way back. Do you mind if we talk about your childhood?"

"I'll save you wear and tear," said Dirk. "I'll give you the facts, and if you want the medical terms I'll give you the conclusions, too–"

"Oh, then, you've had psychiatric treatment." Ellery tried not to look disappointed.

Dirk laughed. "I've tried analysis twice. But it didn't do a damn thing for me but make matters worse. Oh, it wasn't their fault. I couldn't cooperate. Don't ask me why. That's part of it, I suppose."

"Then there's no need to go into it." Ellery set his cup down.

"Wait, I don't mind telling you. It makes some sort of sense." Dirk planted his elbows on his knees and addressed the rug. "I don't have what you'd call a normal background. No sweet dreams for me about my childhood. They're nightmares. It can do things to you, no doubt about it.

"When I was twelve years old my father caught my mother in bed with another man. He beat the guy's brains out with a solid brass lamp he grabbed up from the night table next to the bed.

"He was tried for murder and of course acquitted–any juror would have done the same thing under the same circumstances.

"So that was all right–for him.

"But what happened after wasn't, especially for her and for me. Father had reserved a characteristic punishment for my mother. He refused to divorce her. He made her keep on living with him. In the same community—the same house. And he didn't let a day go by for the rest of their lives without reminding her of what she'd done to him. Her friends wouldn't have anything to do with her, naturally. Her own family threw her over."

Dirk sat back and smiled. "He wasn't going to let her go, you see. That would have been too easy on her—like killing her quick. She had to suffer slow death, *à la chinoise*. She'd dishonored his precious name, disgraced his seminal manhood, and betrayed their codified class … He was quite a guy, my father. I doubt to this day if the embalmer found any blood in his veins. He had that quiet kind of cruelty that's really nasty. Everything under control, you understand, and the amenities of the Southern gentleman observed under all circumstances. When one of that kind gets his knife into you, Brother Elk, you feel pain."

Dirk lit a cigaret and then spent some time crushing it in his saucer. "She tried suicide twice and flubbed it both times. She'd never been taught to do *anything* right, you see. Finally she became a lush, and that's the way I remember my dear mother—a glassy-eyed hag reeking of lavender and old bourbon, staggering around the big house falling-down drunk.

"That's what I grew up with.

"I hated her, and I hated him.

"So maybe Martha is my mother, and I'm my father, or something. And I say to you, as I said to the gentlemen with the couches, 'So what?' Knowing where it comes from hasn't changed a thing. I still get these uncontrollable attacks of jealousy. And I don't mind admitting they scare the hell out of me."

Ellery got out of bed. He said, "Wait, Dirk, till I take my shower," and he went into the bathroom.

When he came out, rubbing his hair, he said, "How are you coming on your new novel?"

Dirk stared. "I'm not."

Ellery began to dress. "Aren't you working at all?"

18

"I sit there eying my typewriter, and it eyes me right back, if that answers your question."

"Much done?"

"I got paralyzed on the excavation."

"What's the matter, isn't it any good?"

"Lordy, no. It's colossal." Dirk laughed.

"Are you still interested in it?"

"What is this, an offer for the first North American serial rights? The idea is as stimulating as it ever was. But I can't seem to get back to it."

"How about professional help?"

"What do you mean?"

"Dirk, your personal problem is beyond me." Ellery tied the second shoe. "If the skull doctors can't do anything about it, I certainly can't. All I can do is suggest a treatment I've found therapeutic in my own lunacies. It's to get out of yourself. A writer does it by writing. Get all wrapped up in a writing problem and drive yourself day and night to fix it on paper."

"I can't, I tell you. I've tried."

"Let's have some breakfast," said Ellery cheerfully. "I have an idea."

Nikki arrived for her secretarial day to find Inspector Queen gone, as usual, and Ellery staring out the window, not as usual.

"Was that Dirk Lawrence I saw shuffling up 87th Street," asked Nikki, "or an unreasonable facsimile thereof?"

"Nikki, grab yourself some coffee and sit down."

"Yes?" said Nikki, not doing either.

"Dirk came up this morning to apologize for last night, and we had a long talk." Ellery gave her a résumé of their conversation. Nikki was silent. "It's obvious that he's in the grip of a dangerous neurosis. I don't like it, Nikki. I don't like it at all."

"Poor Martha," was all Nikki said.

"Yes." Ellery began to stuff a pipe slowly. "For Martha, I'm afraid, the prospects are dim. I'm not sure that even if she left him she'd be in any better case. It might make matters worse at this stage of his phobia. But that's academic. She won't leave him, and we've got to jump off from that."

"Yes," said Nikki. "But what exactly are you afraid of?"

"Violence, especially if Martha gives him provocation."

"He wouldn't!" Nikki sat down with clenched hands.

"Nikki, I've resorted to subterfuge. I've convinced Dirk that his most sensible course is to get back to work on his book."

"He'll never do it."

"That's what he said. But I think he will do it—or keep trying—if there's someone with him constantly whom he likes and trusts, who'll flatter and encourage, take a living interest in what he's doing. In other words, if there's someone at his side to help with his work. The way, for instance, you help me."

Nikki said quietly, "You're farming me out to Dirk Lawrence."

"We've got to have someone on hand when trouble starts, Nikki. Before it starts." Ellery sucked on his pipe. "Nikki Porter, undercover agent. Of course, I neglected to tell Martha that when I phoned her, just before you came in. Dirk was sluggishly interested and rather grateful, and Martha sounded as if I were her patron saint. As far as they're concerned, this is an experiment in trying to get Dirk back to work. You're to act in a Girl Friday capacity, typing for Dirk, telling him what a deathless passage he just dictated, holding his hand when the Muse fails, mixing his cocktails for him—keeping his mind on himself as a writer and off Martha and her imaginary love affairs. "No, wait till I finish, Nikki. Martha insists on your living in. She's going to turn her dressing room into a spare bedroom for you. That's a break, because it puts us on the scene twenty-four hours a day instead of eight. If you agree to do it, you'll have to keep watching for danger signals and make immediate reports to me. If we can keep Dirk harmlessly occupied for long enough, maybe a more permanent course of action will suggest itself.

"And one thing more before you say anything," said Ellery, going over to her. "I wouldn't have cooked this up if I thought I was sending you into personal danger. But that's only one man's guess, and a layman's at that. I've got to leave it up to you, Nikki. In fact, I find myself sort of hoping you'll turn it down."

"All I was trying to say," said Nikki, "was: When do I start?"

Ellery kissed her soberly. "Get into a cab and go right over there."

20

That was a Tuesday. By Friday evening Dirk Lawrence's new secretary was able to report that all was well. In fact, said Nikki, all was so well that she was beginning to wonder if Martha hadn't exaggerated.

"I went over there on Tuesday and Dirk was snoring his head off, catching up on his sleep. So Martha helped me bring some things over from my apartment, and we fixed up the dressing room for me. By that time Dirk had had a shower and changed into clean clothes, and the three of us had a nice objective talk about work and domestic arrangements, and then Martha kissed him and left us in his study, where he works, and we got going.

"He's a dynamo, Ellery. The whole thing seems to have given him a shot in the arm. He had a folder full of notes and we went through them the rest of Tuesday and all day Wednesday, reorganizing his material, discarding a lot of it, making notes of new ideas—I'm really quite impressed. It's going to be a sensational book if it's ever finished. By Wednesday night I was so fagged Martha put her foot down and we knocked off at a reasonable hour. But I didn't let myself fall asleep until I heard Dirk snoring.

"Then yesterday morning we went at it again, and this is the first chance I've had to call. Dirk and Martha are in the tub having a high old time splashing each other, and the three of us are going out to dinner."

"You've seen no sign of anything, Nikki?"

"Not a ripple. He's really thrown himself into this, Ellery. He's trying hard. Martha has her fingers crossed, but she's beginning to look happy again. Oh, I hope this works out."

"Try to arrange a foursome for dinner tomorrow night."

On Saturday night they went to a penthouse restaurant on 59th Street, overlooking Central Park. Dirk ordered breast of guinea hen under glass and French champagne; he was in high spirits. Martha was radiant.

It was Dirk who brought up the subject of the novel. "It's going great," he said. "I never realized before what a difference a skilled literary secretary makes. This must be a real sacrifice for you, Ellery. I can't thank you enough."

"Dedicate the book to me," said Ellery solemnly.

"How about to me?" demanded Nikki.

There was much laughter at their table, in a rather soprano key. El-lery watched Dirk with care. He did not like what he saw, and when they separated in the Lawrence lobby he managed to whisper to Nikki, "Watch out for squalls."

Dirk insisted on working all day Sunday, and on Monday morning, in a new hat and with a light step, Martha left for the theater "to find out," as she grimaced to Nikki, "how much money we lost last week." The Alex Conn play was tapering off after a fairish run, and Martha was looking around for a fall production.

The squall threatened that very morning.

Dirk's exhilaration left the apartment with Martha. His dictation floundered and sank. Nikki tried desperately to resuscitate him. Years of working for a writer had taught her a whole manual of first-aid tricks. She finally gave up.

"You couldn't expect to keep this pace indefinitely, Dirk," she said matter-of-factly. "Let's knock off and take a walk by the river for an hour. I walk Ellery regularly, like a dog."

But Dirk's only response was a mutter as he turned to his portable bar. "I'll be all right. What I need is a drink."

At noon Martha phoned and Nikki felt a great fear. Dirk's mood was unrelieved black by now, and the slow turn of his head as Nikki said, "It's Martha, Dirk," seemed to her to be moved by something lethal.

"Where are you?" Dirk growled.

"At the theater, darling. How are things going?"

"What are you doing?"

"Going over the treasurer's report. Dirk, I think we ought to close— What's the matter?"

"Matter? Nothing. When are you coming home?"

"Right now, darling, if you want me to."

"I don't want you to do anything. You have your work—"

"I'm on my way," said Martha.

With Martha's return, Dirk's mood melted. He dictated at high speed for the rest of the day.

Tuesday was a repetition of Monday.

On Wednesday the inevitable happened. Martha could not come home at the psychological moment. She was tied up at the theater in a tangle of conferences preparatory to closing the play. And this time Dirk's mood froze hard. By the time Martha got back to the apartment he was drunk—so drunk the two women had to help him to bed.

"Poor Nikki," Martha said. The old dead calm had settled over her. "I don't know why you should have to go through all this. It's hopeless."

"It's not hopeless!" Nikki said hysterically. "Not so long as I can get him so drunk he passes out. I'm not going to give up, Martha, I'm *not!*"

She managed to struggle through the rest of the week.

On Sunday Martha and Dirk drove up to Connecticut for dinner with Dirk's publisher, and Nikki felt as if she had been released from a psychopathic ward.

"I don't know what's the matter with him," she told Ellery as they wandered down lower Fifth Avenue towards Washington Square Park in the quiet sun. "He's like two people of opposite temperaments in one body. He'll be way up one minute and in the blackest depths the next. He'll race along dictating really good stuff for fifteen minutes, then all of a sudden he peters out, nothing comes, and he sinks into a kind of witless sluggishness, as if he were doped. Sometimes he's enthusiastic and naive, like a little boy, and in the next breath he's as bitter and disillusioned as a sick old man. I thought you were hard to live with, Ellery, but compared with Dirk you're Little Merry Sunshine."

"I care for this less and less," mumbled Ellery. "How about you pulling out?"

"I can't quit on Martha now, Ellery. And I do have one consolation—I'm not married to him."

Ellery was awakened by his bedside telephone at two o'clock that morning. It was Nikki, and her voice was a quivery whisper. "They got in from Greenwich just after midnight. They were having a terrible fight, Ellery. It seems some other guest—a Book-of-the-Month Club author—was too attentive to Martha, and Dirk got tight and took a poke at him. He's back at the old stand."

"It's hardly credible, but did Martha give him any cause?"

"Martha swears to me she was barely civil to the man. After all, it was in Dirk's publisher's house, and the other man was a guest there, too. He *was* being terribly gallant—acting like the hero of his book, Martha said—but she thought he was making a jackass of himself."

"Where is Dirk now?"

"In bed, asleep. He smashed that gorgeous Wedgwood teapot of Martha's as his exit. If I hadn't ducked, it would have conked me. Martha and I are doubling up in the dressing room tonight. I gave her a pill and finally got her to sleep." Nikki sounded very low.

"Give it up, Nik. You've done your level best. Martha's going to have to work it out for herself."

"No," said Nikki, and he could almost see her chin, "not yet."

The next few days taxed even Nikki's capacity for friendship. She reported that Dirk had stopped work altogether. Nikki would spend an hour or two reading back to him what he had previously got down on paper, trying to "autointoxicate" him, as she put it, into the will to continue. But he would barely pay attention, prowling about the study as if it were a corner of the forest, making frequent stops at the bar, jumping every time the phone rang. Finally he would jam his hat on and stalk from the apartment, to be seen no more until the early hours of the following morning, when Martha would have to undress him and clean him up and haul him into bed with what assistance Nikki could decently provide.

And then the quarrels began again, on the old theme. Martha was seeing too much of her treasurer. Or she had left the apartment half an hour earlier than usual; who was the man? Or—"I stopped into the theater at four-thirty this afternoon and you weren't there. What cocktail bar were you playing footsie in?"

"Martha tries not to lose her temper," said Nikki to Ellery over the phone, "but he keeps needling her until she answers back, and then there's a row. If it were me, I'd break the typewriter over his head. Ellery, I'm afraid I can't give this much more than another day or so—I'll start climbing walls. Would you take one slightly used secretary back tomorrow?"

But tomorrow never came. Nikki failed to appear at the Queen apartment all of the next day. Ellery called the Lawrence apartment several times; there was no answer.

Nikki did not phone until one o'clock the following morning.

She kept her voice low. "I haven't had a minute, Ellery—"

"What's happened, Nikki? I've been worried."

"Yesterday morning—it *was* yesterday, wasn't it? I find myself losing track of time—Martha and I had a long talk. I told her I had every intention of staying as long as I could be of the slightest use, but unless Dirk went back to his novel my position would become impossible. It's a small apartment and when they start fighting I scurry from one hole to another, trying to make myself vanish. I think Martha expected it. She didn't ask me to stay, just kissed me and said that whatever I decided she'd understand, and then she left on some appointment or other without even saying goodbye to Dirk.

"I waited for Dirk to crawl out of bed. It never occurred to me that he was already up and had heard Martha leave. When I got tired of waiting and couldn't find him in the bedroom, I looked in the study and there he was, all dressed, doing something, with his back to me. I was about to deliver my ultimatum, when he turned around and I saw what he was doing."

"What?"

"Cleaning a gun."

Ellery was quiet. Then he said, "What kind of gun?"

"It was a big heavy-looking automatic. It looked a foot long to me. I asked him—laughingly, you understand—what he thought he was doing, and he said something about its being his old Army pistol—"

"A forty-five."

"—and he was cleaning and oiling it, he said, because he'd just got an idea for another detective story and its main plot point had something to do with shooting an automatic from various distances, and a lot of other doubletalk I frankly didn't pay much attention to, I was so petrified. I asked him what about the novel we'd been working on, and he said he was going to drop that for a while and follow this mystery idea of his through—he wasn't sure, he said, if it could be done ... whatever 'it' was. Then he crammed the gun in his pocket—he was wearing an old hunting jacket—and got up and started to leave."

"Poor kid," murmured Ellery.

"You can imagine the thoughts that went through my mind. I could hardly walk out on Martha if Dirk was starting to tote a gun around. Of course, I didn't believe his story about a new mystery idea for a second. I said, 'Where are you going?' and he mumbled something about some friend of his extending the courtesies of a gun club the friend belongs to up in Westchester, and he was going to drive up for some target practice in line with his 'idea'. I thought that was a wild one, too, and more to test him than anything else I asked if I hadn't better go along–to take notes, in case he felt like 'developing' his idea during the day. To my surprise, he said that was a good idea; and–to digest it–we just got in from northern Westchester, where Dirk shot holes in targets at various distances the whole horrible day."

"How was he tonight?"

"Fine. Practically cheerful. Martha was waiting up for us when we got in. He kissed her, asked how her day had been, we all had a nightcap, they went to bed as if nothing had happened, and here I am–and I ask you, Mr. Anthony: Where am I?"

"Did he give you any dictation today on this alleged mystery idea?"

"Yes, notes on a plot. Interesting ones, too. What's my ethical position? After all, you're competitors."

"Did he–or you–tell Martha anything about the day's activities?"

"He did. She went pale, but I don't think he noticed. I managed to talk to her for a couple of minutes in the bathroom before she went to bed. She confirmed the fact that it's his old Army pistol. He hasn't touched it for years, Martha said. She's frightened, Ellery."

"I'd be, too. How good a shot is he?"

"I thought he was Deadeye Dick, but he said he's rusty and his 'tests' weren't 'conclusive' and wouldn't be till he got back his old marksmanship. It seems he was a crack shot in the Army. We're going out to the gun club again tomorrow."

Ellery was silent. Then he said, "Just how determined are you on staying, Nikki?"

"Ellery, how can I leave now? Anyway, maybe it's just what he says. Maybe that's all it is."

"Yes." There was another silence. "If you feel you've got to stick it out, Nikki," he said at last, "don't let him out of your sight. Force him along this new mystery line, whether he wants to follow it up or not. Maybe you can channelize this gun thing off harmlessly. And call me every chance you get."

Ellery was still walking the floor of his study when Inspector Queen turned his alarm off.

"You up at six A.M.?" yawned the Inspector. Then he inhaled. "The millennium! You've already made the coffee."

"Dad."

"What?"

"Do me a favor this morning. Check up on a pistol permit."

"Whose?"

"Dirk Lawrence."

"That fellow?" The Inspector glanced sharply at Ellery, but Ellery's face told nothing. "I'll call you from downtown." The Inspector waited, but Ellery said not another word, and the old gentleman left.

Ellery was awakened by his father's call.

"He has one."

"When was it issued?"

"Last week. Shouldn't it have been? After all, he's a friend of yours." Inspector Queen sounded sarcastic.

"I don't know," said Ellery.

"Think it ought to be revoked?" When Ellery did not reply, the Inspector said, "Ellery, you there?"

"I was just thinking," said Ellery. "If a man is bent on securing possession of a gun, the fact that his license has been revoked isn't going to stop him. And there's no nourishment in jailing a man for using a gun without a license after he's used it. No, Dad, let it ride."

For three days Nikki accompanied Dirk Lawrence to the Westchester gun club, developing a bulky notebook and a slight case of deafness in both ears. Dirk's behavior toward Martha was impeccable, and Martha, reported Nikki, seemed content with small favors. She was very bright and gay when they saw her. The Alex Conn play was in its last week, and she was busy reading manuscripts. At the theater, she explained. She didn't want to drag her work into Dirk's working quarters; the apartment was too small.

"Sounds good," said Ellery.

"It sounds better than it looks," replied Nikki with grimness. "After all, Martha's had training as an actress. But she can't fool me. Her shoulders are developing a permanent hunch. She's waiting for that next blow to fall."

The next blow fell from an unexpected direction, and it struck an unexpected target. For a few days Nikki transcribed her notes and or-

27

ganized them. There was no return to the gun club and the Army auto-matic vanished. Then, after the weekend, Dirk began visiting the New York Public Library at 42nd Street to read up on background for his story. He spent most of Monday and Tuesday away from home. Late on Tuesday afternoon Nikki dropped in to the Queen apartment.

Ellery was shocked. She was haggard; her eyes were wild.

"Nikki, what's the matter?"

"How can you tell?" Nikki laughed hollowly. "Dirk's still at the li-brary and Martha's due home any minute. I can't stay long ... Ellery, I did something today I've never done in my life. I deliberately eavesdropped on a telephone conversation."

"Dirk?"

"Martha."

"Martha?"

"It was this morning," said Nikki, leaning back. "I was up early–I've suffered stupidly from insomnia lately–and I'd just taken my coffee and toast into the study to start typing Dirk's library notes of yesterday when the phone rang. Charlotte–the maid who comes in every day–hadn't got there yet, and Dirk and Martha were still asleep, so I answered. I said hello, and a man's voice said, 'Good morning, Martha darling.'"

Nikki opened her eyes and looked at Ellery as if she expected a suit-able response.

But Ellery said irritably, "What am I supposed to do, phone for the reserves? There must be a hundred men who call Martha darling. I do myself. Who was he?"

Nikki's head rolled. "Give me credit for some sense, Ellery. This wasn't an ordinary, garden-variety darling. This was a darling of a different hue. Rose-colored, if you know what I mean."

"Sorry," said Ellery wearily. "Go on."

"I explained that I wasn't Martha, that Martha was still in bed, and that if he'd leave his number I'd have Martha call back when she woke up. He said never mind, he'd call back himself, and he hung up. And there were no roses in his voice any more when he said it."

"It could have a dozen explanations–"

"Wait. Martha got up about twenty minutes later; I was watching for her. I made sure Dirk was still asleep, then I shut the kitchen door and

28

told her a man had called who wouldn't leave his name and who'd said he was going to call back.

"She went white. When I asked her what was the matter she said it was just nerves, she didn't want to set Dirk off on one of his jealousy tantrums again. She said she thought she knew who it was–some agent who'd been pestering her about a playscript–and that she'd call him back while Dirk was asleep.

"I knew she was lying from the way she waited for me to leave the kitchen before making the call–they have an extension in every room. So I went back to the study, closed the door, and very carefully lifted the receiver on the desk and listened in."

Nikki stopped to moisten her lips.

Ellery said tenderly, "Oh, for the life of a spy. And what did you over-hear?"

"The same man's voice answered. Martha said in a low voice, 'Did you call me just now?' and he said, 'Of course, sweetheart.' Martha told him he shouldn't have phoned, she'd begged him never to phone her apartment. There was absolute terror in her voice, Ellery. She was almost hysterical with fear that Dirk might wake up and listen in. The man kept soothing her, calling her 'dearest' and 'darling,' and he promised that 'from now on' he'd write, not phone."

"Write?" said Ellery. "*Write?*"

"That's what he said. Martha hung up in such a hurry she dropped the phone–I heard the bang."

"Write," muttered Ellery. "I don't get that at all. Unless he *is* an agent, and Martha was telling the truth."

"If he's an agent," said Nikki, "I'm a soubrette."

"His name wasn't mentioned?"

"No."

"What about his voice? Could it have been anyone we've met with or through the Lawrences?"

"It's possible. I thought it sounded familiar, although I couldn't place it."

"What sort of voice was it?"

"Very deep and masculine. A beautiful voice. One of those voices women call sexy."

"Then you shouldn't have had any trouble identifying the body that went with it!"

"Oh, stop being so male, Ellery. The point is, I think Mr. Dirk Lawrence has pushed little Mar into a romance. I'm all for it, mind you, but not while Dirk parks that cannon in the apartment. What do I do now?"

"Did you try talking to Martha again?"

"She didn't give me the chance. She showered, dressed, and was out of there before my hands stopped shaking ... I've been wondering why Martha's acted so strange lately! It was bad enough when Dirk had no grounds. I can imagine what she's going through now."

"So he's going to write," Ellery was mumbling.

"That's what he said. What do I do, snitch the letter?" Nikki sounded bitter.

"You can't do that. But watch for it, Nikki. If possible, find out who the man is. And, of course, do your level best to keep it from Dirk."

Each morning Charlotte, the maid, stopped in the apartment-house lobby to pick up the Lawrence mail from the switchboard and mailbox cubby. On the morning after the mysterious phone call, Nikki beat Charlotte to the cubby by half an hour.

Nikki went through the pile of mail in the elevator. There were five envelopes addressed to "Mrs. Dirk Lawrence" and to "Martha Lawrence." One was a flossy handwritten number from a Park Avenue post-deb friend of Martha's family, but this, Nikki knew, contained nothing more lethal than an invitation to a society wedding. The other four envelopes were typewritten and bore business address imprints in their upper left-hand corners; one was from Bergdorf Goodman.

Nikki riffled through Dirk's mail automatically. One, postmarked Osceola, Iowa, and forwarded by his publisher, was unmistakably a fan letter; there was a bill from Abercrombie & Fitch Company, and a large grand envelope from the Limited Editions Club.

But that was all.

Nikki dropped the letters in the catchall salver on the foyer table, where Charlotte usually left them, and hurried to the study, grateful that the post office still limited itself to a single delivery per day. She felt mean and dirty.

She was to feel dirtier.

Dirk, always a late riser, was still in bed when Nikki finished transcribing his Tuesday's library notes and found herself with nothing to do. Wondering if Martha was awake, she wandered out of the study. Charlotte was in the foyer, vacuuming.

"Mrs. Lawrence? She just got up." Charlotte poked the nozzle of the vacuum cleaner in the direction of the kitchen.

The pile of mail on the foyer table had dwindled.

Nikki went through the swinging kitchen door with a thump. Martha cried out, whirling.

"Nikki!" She tried to laugh. "You startled me."

She had been standing by the dinette table, holding a letter. Unopened envelopes lay on the table.

"I–I thought it was Dirk."

Color came back to her cheeks.

"My goodness, does he affect you that way?" said Nikki cheerily. But she was not feeling at all cheery. Martha had been alone, reading her mail. Why should she have jumped so at an interruption? They were just business letters. *Or were they?* "I think," said Nikki rather faintly, "I'll have a cup of coffee."

As she went to the electric range she saw Martha stuff the envelopes from the table and the letter she had been reading into the pocket of her robe. Martha's movements were hasty and blundering.

"I'd better snag the bathroom before Dirk monopolizes it," Martha said with a shrill laugh. "Once he gets in there …" The rest was lost in the roar of Charlotte's vacuum cleaner as Martha fled.

And there was the letter, on the floor under the dinette table, where it had fallen from Martha's pocket.

Nikki drew a deep breath and pounced.

It was not a business letterhead. There was nothing on the sheet of white paper but a single line of typing. The line had been typed in red.

Thursday, 4 p.m., A

There was nothing to indicate what the typewritten words meant or who had typed them.

The back of the sheet was blank.

31

At the sound of Martha's voice from the foyer Nikki dropped the letter under the dinette table and ran to the cupboard. She was taking down a cup and saucer when the door banged open.

Martha was terrified again. She looked frantically about.

"Nikki, did you happen to see a letter? I must have dropped it—"

"Letter?" said Nikki as casually as she could manage. "Why, no, Mar." She went to the range and picked up the coffeepot.

"Here it is!" The relief in Martha's voice was almost too much to bear. Nikki did not trust herself to turn around. "It fell under the table. It's a—it's a bill I don't want Dirk to know about. You know how he acts when I buy something expensive out of my own money ..."

Nikki murmured something female.

Martha hurried out again.

Nikki telephoned Ellery from the public phone booth in the lobby.

"Now, Nikki," said Ellery, "what's the point of crying?"

"If you could only have seen her, Ellery. Frightened, lying ... It's not like Martha at all. And me, spying on her—lying right back ..."

"You're doing this to help Martha, not hurt her. Tell me what happened."

Nikki told him.

"You didn't see the envelope?"

"I must have, when I looked over the mail in the elevator this morning. But I have no way of telling which one the letter was in."

"Too bad. The envelope might have—"

"Wait," said Nikki. "I do know."

"Yes?" said Ellery eagerly.

"The message on the sheet of paper—the enclosure—was typed on the red part of a black-and-red ribbon. I remember now that on one of the envelopes I handled this morning Martha's name and address were typed in red, too."

"Red typing on the *envelope?*" Ellery sounded baffled. "You don't happen to recall the name of the business firm imprinted on the upper left corner?"

"I think it was an air-conditioning company, but I don't remember the name."

32

"Air-conditioning company ... Not a bad dodge. Any envelope like that would naturally be taken to contain an advertising mailing piece. So if Dirk happened to get to the mail first—"

"Ellery, I've got to get back upstairs. Dirk may be up."

"You say, Nikki, this took place in the kitchen?"

"Yes."

"I seem to recall a wastepaper basket near the dinette alcove. Is the basket still there?"

"Yes."

"She may have dropped the envelope into it. She'd have no reason to be careful about the envelope. Did you look in the basket?"

"I didn't look for the envelope at all!"

"Naturally," soothed Ellery. "But it won't hurt to look, Nikki. I'd very much like to examine that envelope."

"All *right*," said Nikki, and she used the phone for punctuation.

She brought him the envelope at noon.

"We needed some more carbon paper, so I told Dirk I'd have lunch out today. I'll have to cab right back, Ellery, or they may suspect something. It was in the wastepaper basket."

"Lucky!"

The manila envelope was of the clasp type, about five inches by eight. A strip of heavy adhesive paper had been used for sealing above the clasp. On the face, typed in red, were the words "Mrs. Dirk Lawrence" and the Beekman Place address. The inscription in the upper left corner was THE FROEHM AIR-CONDITIONER COMPANY; the address was The 45th Street Building, 547 Fifth Avenue, New York. The entire left side of the envelope was decorated with a cartoonical drawing of a heat-prostrated family, over the legend: *Why Live in a Turkish Bath This Summer?*

"This is a current city-wide promotion campaign," Ellery said, turning the envelope this way and that. "Dad received a similar envelope last week, enclosing a mailing piece on the new Froehm air-conditioner."

"Was the address in red?"

"Black. This is a puzzler, Nikki."

"How do you mean?"

33

"There was more in this envelope than that single sheet of paper you saw Martha reading."

Nikki stared at it. "It does look as if it had contained something bulky." The empty envelope was not flat. A rectangle of creases back and front held it in a three-dimensional shape. "Maybe the pamphlet about the air-conditioner, although how he got a letter into a business firm's envelope—"

"The Froehm brochure was one of those unfolding broadsides, which fold down into a flat piece. Nothing that flat ever made these creases, Nikki. These were made by something about three eighths of an inch thick."

"Sounds almost like a book—"

"A booklet. In fact, these dimensions suggest a twenty-five-cent reprint edition, a paperback. You saw nothing like that in Martha's hand, or on the table, while she was reading the message?"

"No. But she might have slipped it into the pocket of her robe when she opened the envelope. The robe she was wearing has big patch pockets, and they're usually full of things."

"Are you up to a little more snoopery, Nikki?"

Nikki looked at him. "You want me to search for the booklet."

"It would help."

"All right," said Nikki.

"Look for a paperback about four inches by seven, and about three eighths of an inch thick."

"Martha's hardly likely to leave it lying around. That means I may have to go into her purse ... her bureau ..."

Ellery said nothing.

"I wish," began Nikki, but she bit off the rest of it; and after a moment she said, "Do you really think it's a—it's an affair?"

"Looks like it," said Ellery.

"*Thursday, 4 P.M.* That's tomorrow afternoon." Nikki clenched her gloved hands. "Why does she take such a foolish chance? Hasn't she had enough of Dirk's jealousy? Why doesn't she divorce him and then do what she pleases? I'd like to get my hands on that 'A'—whoever he is!"

"*A?*" said Ellery.

"The '*A*' that signed the message, Ellery. I've been beating my brains out trying to think of some man she knows whose first name begins with

34

an *A*, but I can't come up with anyone but Alex Conn and Arthur Morvyn. And Alex is a fairy and Art Morvyn has been directing Broadway plays for forty years and must be seventy if he's a day. It can't be either of them."

"The *A* isn't the initial of a name, Nikki."

"It isn't?"

"Signatures are almost invariably dropped below the message, on a line to themselves. It's true this is a short message and the writer might have added his initial on the same line because there's so little to it. But then he'd probably have separated the *m* of *p.m.* from the *A* by a dash. You told me there was a comma after *p.m.*"

"That's right."

"Then the *A* was part of the message, not a sign-off." Ellery shrugged. "That's confirmed by inference. The message undoubtedly refers to an appointment. There are two major elements to any meeting—the time and the place. The time is given as tomorrow at four. The likelihood, then, is that the *A* refers to the place."

"I'm relieved," said Nikki dryly. "I thought you were going to say it's symbolism."

"Symbolism?"

"A nice scarlet letter *A à la* Nathaniel Hawthorne. I just don't know what to make of it, Ellery. It's so hard to see Martha in the role of Hester Prynne! She's just not the adulteress type."

"Is there one?" inquired Ellery. "Anyway, we'll know soon enough what *A* stands for. Probably a primitive code. What you've got to do tomorrow, Nikki, is tie Dirk in knots for the whole afternoon. Keep him in that apartment if you have to make love to him. If he insists on going out, delay him on some pretext to make sure Martha gets away."

"What are you going to do, Ellery?"

"Make like a private eye and trail Martha to *A*—wherever *A* is."

"Suppose she leaves the house in the morning?"

"We'll have to prearrange a code of our own. Do your best to find out about when she intends to leave the apartment. Phone me forty-five minutes before. It doesn't matter what you say to me when you call. The mere fact that you're phoning will be my tipoff."

B ...

Nikki phoned at twenty minutes after eleven Thursday morning. She was phoning, she told Ellery, to call off their "tentative lunch date." Dirk had his plot pretty well organized and he was starting to dictate manuscript. He planned to work right through the day.

"Wonderful," said Ellery. "Let me talk to him, Nikki."

Dirk sounded energetic. "Hi, Ellery! I think I've hit pay dirt in this one. I hope you don't mind Nikki's breaking your date."

"Think nothing of it. I understand you're really on fire, Dirk."

"Don't hex me, son. I have to nurse these spells." Dirk laughed.

"How true," mourned Ellery; and he hung up and ran.

At a few minutes past noon Ellery's cab was cruising through Beekman Place for the third time when he saw Martha Lawrence come out of the apartment house and step into a taxi waiting at the curb. She was dressed in a mousy brown suit with black accessories and a large-brimmed black hat with a thick-meshed nose veil. The hat overshadowed her face.

Martha's cab drove west to Park Avenue and stopped before the entrance of the Marguery. She got out, paid her driver, and entered the Open Air Pavilion.

Ellery waited two minutes. Then he went in, too.

Martha was seated at a choice table with a woman. The woman was gross and dowdy, about fifty-five years old. One of her legs protruded from under the cloth; it was elephantine.

Ellery selected a table some distance away, a little behind and to the right of the two women. The distance did not bother him; he had sharp eyes.

They had cocktails. Martha had a single whisky sour, her companion three martinis, which she tossed off in rapid succession. Ellery sighed; it looked like a long lunch.

He had to be on the alert. Martha was uneasy. She kept looking around unexpectedly, as if searching for someone she knew. Ellery worked first with the menu, then with a copy of the *Herald Tribune* which he had picked up on his way crosstown.

It was the dowdy woman's treat. She had a trick of leaning toward Martha, her oily lips apart, in an attitude of rapture at Martha's every word. She was all adoration.

Selling something, Ellery decided.

She was an old hand at it, too. She did not produce her wares until the dessert, and then carelessly.

It was a thick book of typewriter paper bound in bright pink covers and held together by fancy brass pins.

As Martha riffled it and then dropped it into her black envelope bag, the woman continued to chatter away.

She was an agent peddling a playscript. Either by accident or design, Martha had managed a legitimate excuse to explain her afternoon's absence.

At five minutes of two Martha glanced at her wristwatch, said something with a smile, and rose. Caught by surprise, the agent looked grim. But she immediately beamed again, made an eager remark, waved a meaty arm at the waiter, dropped a ten-dollar bill on the table, and was scrambling after Martha in a triumph of integrated motion. She crowded Martha out and onto the sidewalk, clutching and talking all the while. Not until Martha's cab door had slammed and the cab was rolling off did she stop talking, and then her look became grim again and she climbed wearily into another taxi.

But by that time Ellery was turning from Park Avenue into a crosstown street in Martha's wake.

Martha's cab discharged her at the corner of Fifth Avenue and 49th Street.

She went into Saks.

For the next hour and a half Ellery trailed her through the big store. She made numerous purchases–toilet water, stockings, lingerie, two pairs of shoes, some summer sportswear. But she made her selections without interest, almost listlessly. Ellery had the feeling that she was marking time, perhaps setting up the corroboration of a second alibi announced in advance. She took none of her purchases with her.

Before leaving the store, she paused on the main floor to buy some men's socks and handkerchiefs. These, too, she ordered sent. Ellery contrived to pass close by when the clerk was writing in his sales book, hoping he might catch the name and address of the man for whom she was buying the socks and handkerchiefs. He was successful but untriumphant: they were to be sent, he heard Martha instruct the salesman, to "Mr. Dirk Lawrence" at the Beekman Place address on her Charga-Plate.

Ellery felt that this tactic was not worthy of such a candid person as Martha. It suggested too depressingly the veteran wool-puller.

She left Saks-Fifth Avenue at nineteen minutes to four, ignored a taxi discharging a passenger, and began to walk north.

A, then, was nearby.

Martha passed St. Patrick's Cathedral, Best's, Cartier's, Georg Jensen's.

A few minutes later she crossed Fifth Avenue and walked rapidly west.

At one minute to four, Martha went into the A— Hotel.

The A— Hotel was an old hotel with a distinguished past. Its trade was largely transient, but it had a hard core of celebrated residents which gave it a romantic flavor. It was a favorite hideaway dining and meeting place for the more literate habitués of Broadway, and it was exactly the sort of place where Martha Lawrence might be expected to go.

Ellery strolled into the lobby, wondering if he and Nikki had not misjudged Martha after all.

Martha's back was on view at the other end of the lobby. A tall man with a very dark tan had jumped up from an overstuffed chair and was talking to her.

Ellery walked over to the newsstand and began to finger a copy of *Ellery Queen's Mystery Magazine.*

The lobby was dim after the bright afternoon sunshine and he had to squint to make out the tall man's features. What he could distinguish under the tan seemed rather heavily handsome. Martha's companion wore his thick blond or gray hair–in the poor light, and at that distance, Ellery could not determine which it was–with a dash. The lounge suit was beautifully draped; there was a spring aster in the lapel. The Homburg had swash.

The man was not young.

As he talked, he kept smiling.

The fellow talked with a technique. His eyes never left Martha's upturned little face, as if he had starved for a sight of her and now could not restrain his hunger. His hand hovered about Martha's upper arm as he talked.

There was something teasingly familiar about him–his brilliant smile, the trained slouch, the way his big shoulders filled his jacket, his air of unconquerable self-assurance. Ellery was positive he had met the man somewhere, or seen him around town.

Suddenly Martha walked off. She opened a door off the lobby and disappeared. Ellery moved a bit. It was a ladies' room. The man's eyes followed her all the way in.

Ellery placed a quarter and a dime down on the newsstand counter and strolled off reading the magazine. As he neared the elevators, the tall man put on his Homburg, settling it with care on his head. He arranged it at a jaunty angle. Then he walked over to the elevators, looking up at the bronze indicators over the doors. He seemed pleased with himself; his cheeks were going in and out in a soft whistle.

Ellery burrowed into the corner of a settee which faced the elevators, under a luxuriant philodendron.

It was blond hair, not gray. The temples were gray.

He was in his fifties and not making the mistake of trying to look thirty-five. A Man of Distinction, say forty-five. A model, however, not the original. The angle of his hat betrayed him.

One of the elevator doors opened. The man stepped into the elevator and said, "Six, please." The voice was deep, richly colored, and resonant, with the merest British tinge.

The voice did it. Now the angle of the hat, the beautifully tailored suit, the aster, and the barbershop tan all fitted.

The fellow was an actor.

Legitimate theater, of course.

That's where I've seen him, thought Ellery. But who is he?

Four other people got into the elevator, including a woman. There was no sign of Martha.

Ellery got up and stepped into the elevator, too. He stepped in sidewise, removing his hat as he did so. It shielded his face long enough to allow him to turn naturally and face the door. The tall man was at the rear of the elevator, his Homburg over his heart; he was humming.

Ellery got off at the fifth floor.

He ran up the emergency staircase to the sixth in time to hear the elevator door clang. He waited three seconds, then he opened the exit door and stepped out.

The main corridor was at right angles to the bank of elevators. Ellery walked past the intersection. Far down the corridor the tall man was unlocking a door.

When he heard the door close, Ellery turned back and hurried up the long corridor.

The room was 632.

He kept going to the end of the corridor, where it was met by another cross-corridor. The short corridor was empty.

Ellery waited at the intersection.

Five minutes later he heard the distant rattle of the elevator door and he stepped back out of sight. He heard the elevator door open and close.

After a moment he held his hat before his face, as if he were about to put it on, and walked rapidly across the intersection.

It was Martha.

She was hurrying up the main corridor, searching the door numbers.

Ellery remained on the other side of the cross-corridor, just out of view.

A few seconds later he heard a series of light, rapid knocks. A door opened at once.

"What held you up, darling?" An actor, all right. And a leading man, at that.

"Hurry!" Martha's familiar voice, unfamiliarly breathless.

The door slammed.

After a moment Ellery heard the lock turn over.

He went back downstairs and waited near the desk for a couple to check in and follow a bellhop.

"Hello, Ernie."

The desk clerk looked startled. "Mr. Queen!" he said. "I thought you'd taken your trade elsewhere. Checking in to meet a deadline?"

40

"Mine died some time ago," said Ellery. "No, Ernie, I'm looking for information."

"Oh," said the clerk, lowering his voice. "Your alter ego, eh?" Like all old employees of the A— Hotel, he had long since absorbed its literary atmosphere. "Man-hunt?"

"Well, it's a man," said Ellery. "The man in six-thirty-two. What's his name, Ernie?"

"Mr. Queen, we're not supposed to give out—"

"Let's say you were looking over the registration cards and began muttering to yourself?"

"Yes." The clerk coughed and moved over to the card file hanging on the wall beside the desk. "Six-thirty-two ... Checked in at one-five P.M. today ..." He looked around. "You won't care for this, Mr. Queen. He's registered as George T. Spelvin, East Lynne, Oklahoma."

"Typical actor's humor. Come on, Ernie, you know who he is. You know every actor in the Lambs."

The desk clerk straightened the pen in its holder. "You flatter me," he murmured, "and I like it. The Westphalian is Van Harrison. What's the lay, chief?"

"Guard your language. No, it's nothing you can peddle to the columns, worse luck. I spotted him, thought he looked familiar, and wondered who he was. Thanks a lot." Ellery grinned and went out.

But on the street his grin faded.

"Van Harrison." He found himself saying it aloud.

He stopped in a Sixth Avenue drugstore to phone Nikki. Dirk Lawrence answered.

"Hi, there. How's it coming?"

"Pretty good, pretty good." Dirk sounded absent.

"Any chance of my borrowing my secretary for this evening, chum?"

"You're damn decent to do this for me, Ellery. How much will you take for her contract?"

"That isn't answering my question."

"I guess it can be arranged, old boy—Martha and I are invited to the Le Fleurs' for dinner, and that means black tie, a butler with palsy, and Charades in the drawing room afterward. I'm beginning to hope Martha doesn't come home at all."

41

"That's a switch," laughed Ellery. "Let me speak to Nikki."

Nikki said, "And how has *your* day been?"

"Surprisingly surprising. How about meeting me for dinner?"

"Why, Mr. Q."

"Make it Louis and Armand's as close to seven as you can get away. Don't keep me waiting too long, because I'll be at the bar, and you know how conscientious Pompeia is."

"No, but I know you. Three drinks and you're the Human Fly."

"I'm climbing no walls this night. It's serious business, Nikki."

Nikki said fervently, "I can hardly wait," and hung up.

Nikki said, "Van Harrison," as if it were the name of a loathsome disease. "What can she see in him? I thought he was dead."

"Unkind, Nikki," murmured Ellery. "I can testify that Mr. Harrison is no corpse. And—I'm afraid—so can Martha."

"But he's an *old man.*"

"Not so old. It wasn't more than a dozen or so years ago that he was jamming the theaters with standees and having to fight his way out of the stage door. That profile still packs a wallop, Nikki. Terrific personality."

"I could strangle him," said Nikki, panting. "Martha in a hotel room! Where'd she ever meet him?"

"Broadway is a small town. Maybe he applied for a part in one of her productions. I made a few inquiries at the Lambs after I phoned and I'm told he's seen every once in a while still trying to break down the Broadway ban on him. I don't suppose you remember that. He went on a prolonged drunk in his last starring play for Avery Langston, and Langston had to close down at the height of a run. Harrison hasn't had a job on Broadway since. That must have been ten or twelve years ago."

"Then what's he living on, his old press notices?"

"He doesn't have to work at all. He made a fortune in his lush years, but you know actors. He still takes an occasional radio and TV job, and once in a while he gets a character part in some film. It's probably keeping him alive. That magic voice and romantic profile of his will lure women of Martha's age when he's tripping over his beard."

"But *Martha*."

"What about Martha?" said Ellery coldly. "What's so different about Martha? She's in her middle thirties, she has a husband who's making her life hell with his crazy jealousy, she has no children and no family to hold her back, and she's stagestruck. Why, Martha's duck soup for an operator like Harrison! He can give her what Dirk can't, or won't—flattery, attention, mastery, glamor. He can give her happiness, Nikki, even if it's only a cheap substitute in a hotel room."

"But Martha's always been so level-headed. Can't she see he's a phony?"

"Who's real in this world? And maybe he's in love with her. Martha isn't so hard to take."

Nikki was silent.

"In other words," said Ellery after a while, "it's one hell of a mess, and I'm for getting out."

"Not now."

"Now is the only time. Later we may not be able to."

"Not while it's going on." Nikki shivered. "Not while there's a chance of Dirk's finding out."

"I take it, then, you're for continuing to hole up at the Lawrences'."

"Ellery, I have to."

Ellery grunted. "Why did I ever let myself be conned into this?" He kept drumming on the cloth. Nikki watched him anxiously. "Of course, the sensible thing is a girl-to-girl talk. After all, there is the basis for it, Nikki. We came into this because Martha said Dirk was being jealous for no reason. The situation has changed. He now—fortunately still unknown to him—has the best reason in the world. She's cut the ground away from under us. If we're to continue to help her—"

"We'll have to do it in spite of her."

Ellery threw up his hands. "Every time I make a constructive suggestion—!"

"Look, dear," said Nikki, "I know women and you don't. If I told Martha what we know and pleaded with her to stop before something drastic happens, she'd deny the whole thing. She'd deny it because she thinks she's madly in love. Besides making up some embarrassing fairy tale to explain why she's meeting this Harrison man in

43

hotel rooms, she'd hate me for knowing it, I'd have to leave, and that would be that."

Ellery grumbled something.

"If Martha were ready to come clean, Ellery, she'd have walked into that hotel room a free woman instead of sneaking in like a tart. The fact is, she's decided to have an affair while maintaining the fiction that she's trying to save her marriage."

"But that's illogical!"

"When a good woman falls, Mr. Queen, you can throw your logic down the johnny. Ellery, I'm sorry I dragged you into this. Why don't you just forget it and let me blunder along in my own way?"

"Very clever," snarled Ellery. "All right, we try to save them in spite of themselves. And we'll wind up right where we belong, behind the nearest eight-ball!"

Nikki pressed his hand below the table. "You darling," she said tenderly.

So after they had eaten the salad that was not on the menu, Ellery complained further: "The thing that bothers me most is that we can't plan ahead. There's nothing to plan. It's like being asked to watch for a firebug loose in an ammunition dump on a moonless night. All I can do is stumble after Martha in the dark and hope I'll be there to step on the match before everything goes boom."

"I know, dear heart …"

"You hijack that next letter, Nik. You'll have to read it this time before Martha does—she won't be so obliging as to drop it on the kitchen floor again. It will probably be in a business envelope, too. It's a good dodge and the kind of pattern that, once established, is pretty sure to be followed."

"But he wouldn't use the envelope of that air-conditioner company again," objected Nikki. "That would be dangerous."

"It would," said Ellery, "therefore the second note will come in an altogether different envelope."

"But how will I know which one?"

"I can't help you. You may have to steam open every business letter addressed to Martha. And, since we've agreed to play blindman's buff all around, I suppose I'd better warn you not to get caught at it, even by the maid."

Nikki gulped. "I'll try to be careful."

"Yes," said Ellery without mercy. "Louis! Where's our *tetrazzini?*"

Nikki called the Queen apartment late Saturday afternoon to say that she was free for the evening, if anybody was interested. Inspector Queen, who took the message, had to have it translated.

"It means she's got something," said Ellery with excitement. "Give me that phone! Nikki, well?"

"Well, what?" said Nikki's voice. "Do we have a date, or don't we?"

"Can't talk?"

"No."

"The apartment. Any time you can make it."

"What's going on here?" demanded his father when Ellery hung up. "What are you two up to?"

"Nothing good," said Ellery.

"Anything in my line?"

"Heaven forbid."

"You'll get around to me yet," said the Inspector cheerfully. "You always do."

Nikki showed up a few minutes past nine, looking more dead than alive.

"Excuse us?" said Ellery politely, and he shut the study door on the Inspector, who was watching Sid Caesar in the living room. "I've got your drink ready, Nik. Kick off your shoes, lie down, and give out."

Nikki sank back on the couch, wiggling her toes, set the highball glass untouched on the floor, and addressed the ceiling. "I am now," she announced, "the female Jimmy Valentine of my darning and knitting circle. I don't suppose you want the technical details?"

"Correct," said Ellery. "Results are all that interest me. And they were?"

"You have no heart."

"This is a heartless racket, child. Well?"

"The letter came in this morning's mail," said Nikki dreamily. "There were three business-type envelopes, but I didn't have to steam open all three. I spotted the right one at a glance."

"You did?" Ellery was astonished. "Froehm again?"

"No. This was an ordinary long white envelope with the return address of a business firm named Humber & Kahn, Jewelers. But the ad-

45

dress was The 45th Street Building, 547 Fifth–same as the air-conditioner outfit, please note. And– get this ..."

"Oh, come on!"

"Martha's name and address were typewritten *in red again.*"

Ellery stared. "Funny."

"Stupid, I calls it. That red typing is a dead giveaway all by itself, if Dirk should happen to notice it a few times. Luckily, he almost never gets to the mail first."

"Go on," muttered Ellery. "What did this message say?"

"It said–in the same red-ribbon typing, by the way–'Monday comma 3 P.M. comma *B*.'"

"*B?*"

"*B.*"

C ...

Monday was a fine day for shadowing if you were an otter. The rains came and went all day, mischievously, sometimes a drizzle and at others a rattling shower that drove people off the streets. As usual in New York, at the first hint of moisture empty taxicabs became rarer than a traffic officer's smile.

Ellery spent the whole morning and part of the afternoon shivering in his raincoat under a candy-store awning across the street from a shabby apartment house in Chelsea. Martha had found a play for the fall and she was going over it with the author, a young housewife who had written it between diaper-washings and sessions over the range.

It looked like a long wait.

It was.

Martha apparently had lunch there. For noon came, and one o'clock, and one-thirty, and there was still no sign of her.

At one-forty-five Ellery began to hunt for a cab. It took him twenty minutes to capture one, and even then he almost lost it when the driver learned that he was expected to wait indefinitely around the corner with his flag down. A five-dollar bill secured his loyalty.

Martha emerged at twenty-five minutes past two, unfurling an umbrella. She hurried in her plastic overshoes toward Eighth Avenue, looking around anxiously every few steps. Ellery, keeping his head down and his collar up, followed on the opposite side of the street, trying successfully to look like a miserable man.

At that, he had a close call. A cab appeared from nowhere, discharged a passenger, engulfed Martha, and was off before Ellery could reach the corner. He had to sprint to his waiting taxi. Fortunately, Martha's cab was held up two blocks south by a red light. Ellery's driver, sensing adventure, caught up at 15th Street.

"Where's she headed, buddy?" he asked.

"Just follow her."

"You her husband?" the driver said wisely. "I had a wife once. Take it from me, Mister, it don't pay to knock yourself out. That's the way I always figure. Give the other guy the headache. Why fight City Hall?"

"There they go, damn it!"

"Keep your pants on," soothed the driver; and they were off again.

Martha's cab turned left on 14th Street and began the long crawl east. Ellery nibbled his nails. Traffic was heavy and visibility poor. It was raining hard again. Where was she going?

At Union Square he half-expected the cab they were following to head north. But instead it turned south into Fourth Avenue.

The secondhand bookshops swam by.

Was she going down Lafayette Street? That way lay Police Headquarters. It seemed improbable.

At Astor Place, behind Wanamaker's, Martha's cab turned into Cooper Square and cut across to Third Avenue. It settled into a sedate southward journey under the El.

Monday, 3 P.M., B ... B for *Brooklyn*? Was she bound for the Williamsburg Bridge and the East River?

And suddenly it came to Ellery that, where Martha's cab had turned into Third Avenue to head south, Third Avenue ceased to exist. Where Third Avenue met 4th Street, it became The Bowery.

B for *Bowery* it was.

But The Bowery ran all the way down to Chatham Square. She could hardly be peering out of her window hoping to spot Van Harrison on some unnamed street corner in the dingy gloom of the El. It had to be a specific place on The Bowery. A Bowery-Something ... Bowery Mission!

It was not The Bowery Mission. It proved to be 267 Bowery, and it caught the philosopher driving Ellery's cab as much by surprise as his passenger ...

Near Houston Street Martha's taxi, treacherously, made a full turn under the El. Martha jumped out, the door of a cab parked on the east side of the street popped open to receive her, and the last Ellery saw of her was a glimpse through the window of Van Harrison embracing her as their cab shot away from the curb, made a quick turn, and disappeared up a side street; By the time Ellery's driver extricated himself from a tangle of northbound traffic and duplicated the maneuver, the enemy was out of sight.

"Why didn't you tell me she was meeting him in front of Sammy's Bowery Follies?" demanded the driver in an injured tone. "Then I'd been prepared."

"Because Sammy's Bowery Follies begins with an *S*," snapped Ellery, "and if that's cricket it ought to be baseball. Stop at a drugstore so I can use a phone, then take me up to West 87th Street."

"With what's on the meter already," said the driver unhappily, "that's going to use up a good hunk of the fin." And there was no further communion between them.

Nikki managed to get away late Monday evening, and she burst into the Queen apartment with a "Well?" that faltered at sight of the Inspector.

"It's all right, Nikki," growled Ellery, "I've told Dad all about it. This looks like a long job. It was Sammy's Bowery Follies, Bowery and Houston, with the 'Sammy' apparently canceled out. In short, I lost them. What time did Miss Prynne get home?"

"At the usual time. For dinner." Nikki sank into a chair. "*B* ... Bowery."

"I think you two ought to have your heads examined," exclaimed Inspector Queen. "Mixing up in an adultery case! Anyway it turns out, Nikki, you're going to catch the dirty end of the stick. And don't give me any taffy about friendship. In an adultery case there's no friends, just subpoenas. I've already notified my son what I think of *his* judgment. And now, if you can bear it, I'm going to bed."

"But why Bowery Follies?" asked Nikki, when the Inspector's door had thundered. "What on earth were they doing there, Ellery?"

"Harrison's an actor. The ham instinct. It's romantic to meet on The Bowery and go scudding off in the rain. Gives that preliminary zing to the big scene. After all, there isn't much variety in hotel rooms, or what usually goes on in them under these circumstances." Ellery packed a pipe, viciously.

"Then you think they were going ..."

"I assure you Martha didn't jump into his taxi to discuss a casting problem. The last I saw, Harrison had a stranglehold on her collarbone. I leave it to you what their destination was."

"The A— again?" asked Nikki in a small voice.

"Not the A—. I phoned Ernie at the desk. Harrison checked out Friday morning and he hasn't been back since. It was an academic call. Does it really matter what hotels they use?" Nikki did not reply. "How did our heroine act when she got home?"

"Subdued."

"Huh!"

"And ... very nice to Dirk."

"Of course."

"Kept talking through dinner about the play she's taken an option on. And about this Ella Greenspan, the young housewife who wrote it."

"She also contrived to give the impression that she spent not only the morning but the entire afternoon with the precocious Mrs. Greenspan? Came directly home from Chelsea, and so on?"

"Well ... yes."

"And what's on her agenda for tonight?"

"Martha's reading Dirk the play."

"Touching. By the way, how was Dirk?"

"Very interested. They went right into the study after dinner. That's how I was able to get away. Dirk asked me to stay and listen in, but Martha seemed to want him to herself, so ... Well, I said I'd some things to buy at the drugstore. I suppose Martha's afraid of me these days."

"I'm beginning," remarked Ellery, "not to care a great deal for your Martha Lawrence, Nikki."

Nikki nibbled her lip.

"But the situation does have its element of repulsive fascination. It's sort of like living in a keyhole." Then Ellery blew an apologetic cloud of smoke and laid his pipe down. Nikki was looking so miserable that he pulled her over to him. "I'm sorry. I guess I'm not used to this kind of case. Why are you getting up?"

"No reason. I want a cigaret."

Ellery lit one for her. She returned to her own chair.

"You hate me."

"I hate men!"

"Now, be reasonable, Nikki. It takes two to build a love nest. I hold no brief for Harrison, but Martha's not exactly jail bait. She's old enough to be held responsible for her acts."

"All *right*," cried Nikki. "Can't we get back to the point? Do you want me to keep steaming open business envelopes?"

"I want you to come home. But if you won't—yes." Ellery picked up his pipe again. "By the way, today—we may say with some justification—we've progressed."

"In which direction?" asked Nikki bitterly.

"Exactly. But that's not what I mean. The pattern's beginning to show.

"Harrison," said Ellery, "has apparently worked out a melodramatic but effective enough scheme for having his pigeon and eating it, too. Different meeting places each time, and then away to the day's nest. The only point of contact necessary under this layout is a time designation, place being expressed in code, and the whole luscious package enclosed in an innocuous business envelope. With Martha coming and going at all hours on legitimate business, and Dirk used to it—even though he breaks out in occasional rashes of jealousy-it's not a bad set-up at all.

"Harrison's really reduced the danger of discovery to a minimum.

"The code itself," continued Ellery to the wall, since Nikki was looking there, too, "presents certain primitive points of interest. *A* comes first and turns out to represent the A— Hotel. *B* comes second and we find it indicates Bowery Follies. We may infer, then, that the next code letter will probably be *C*, and that *C* will stand for Carnegie Hall, or Coney Island, or somewhere in Central Park; that *D* will follow *C* and designate the *Daily News* building or Danny's Hideaway; and so on. What Harrison will do when he exhausts the alphabet, assuming he can get away with it that long," said Ellery gravely, "heaven only knows. Probably start working backwards from Z."

"Games," said Nikki. "Games!"

"But now the question: How did Martha know that *A* didn't stand for the Astor, or the Art Students' League, or the American Museum of

Natural History? And *B*—why not Bellevue Hospital, or the Broadway Tabernacle, or Battery Park? The *B* was unqualified, except for time; so was the *A*. How did she know?

"The answer is that the initial-letter element of the code must be part of it only. The master key of the code must specify which *A*-place of all the *A*-places in New York the letter *A* in the code is to designate. Harrison has one copy of the decoding instrument, Martha the other. When she gets a message designating *C*, she'll simply look up *C* in her copy, and she's away."

"That first envelope," said Nikki, "retaining the shape of some booklet!"

"Nice work," grinned Ellery. "Have you kept looking for it?"

"Well—yes."

"Not, I gather, with the enthusiasm its importance warrants. You see how exacting detective work is, Nikki. You've got to find that booklet. It's probably a guidebook of some sort to places of interest in New York City. With it we'll know where they'll meet *before* they meet. The advantages are self-evident."

"Tonight," said Nikki through her teeth, "you're talking like Professor Queen, and I don't appreciate it. I'll find the damned thing! What's that you've got there?"

"This?" Ellery looked up from a little black notebook he had taken from his breast pocket. "This is my case book."

"Case book?"

"Times, dates, where they meet, where they go, what they do, to the best of my knowledge and belief ... Who knows? It may come in handy."

Nikki went off drooping.

While waiting for the next rendezvous, Ellery thought he might as well settle a point or two.

He spent all of Tuesday, Wednesday, and Thursday in an apparently aimless round of phone calls and visits to various Broadwayites of his acquaintance. He lunched at Sardi's and the Algonquin, had dinner at Lindy's and Toots Shor's, dropped in at 21 and the Stork, ate a midnight snack at Reuben's, and by Thursday evening he was far fuller of good food than of digestible information. He might have done better pumping the columnists, but he made broad detours whenever he spotted one. Expert of the painless exploratory technique as he was, he did not dare risk a consultation with the specialists. In fact, the newspapers these days gave him the horrors, and he scanned Winchell and Lyons and Sullivan and the rest with the fears of a man of much guiltier conscience.

The friendship of Martha Lawrence and Van Harrison was of very recent date. No one Ellery spoke to had ever seen them together, or even separately in the same place, until a few weeks before. On that occasion—Ellery's informant was Maud Ashton, an old character woman with the acquaintanceship of Elsa Maxwell and the certified circulation of *Life*—they had both attended the all-night telethon emceed by a round robin of TV comedians in the interest of the recent blood-plasma drive. Martha had been there as one of the Broadway celebrities to supervise the studio blood donations, Harrison as a personality of the theater to entertain the television audience. He had given his famous imitation of John Barrymore, and it had netted so much blood for the drive that Harrison remained for the rest of the night, assisting Mrs. Lawrence.

"They made such a handsome pair," Miss Ashton smiled. "I wonder if her husband was at his set."

"Why, what do you mean?" asked Ellery.

"Not a blinking thing, Ellery, curse the luck. Of course, Van's an old reprobate who'll play Sextus seven nights a week, but everybody knows little Martha Lawrence is as faithful as Lucrece, and I can't see Dirk Lawrence in the role of Tarquin, can you? Sextus … You know, considering the plot line, that's awfully cute?"

If Maud Ashton was still thinking such noble thoughts, hope was not dead.

The second point advanced Ellery no further than the first. He visited 547 Fifth Avenue on Friday and discovered from the directory in the lobby that the Froehm Air-Conditioner Company occupied Suite 902-912, while Humber & Kahn, jewelers, had their showroom in 921. The occurrence of the ninth floor in the case of both envelopes suggested a certain line of investigation, and Ellery duly pursued it after six o'clock on Saturday afternoon, when most of the tenants of the building were gone. But he did not come empty-handed. First, on Saturday morning, he made one of his rare excursions to Brooklyn, to the home of an old man who owned a world-famous collection of theatrical photographs. Here, after representing himself as a feature writer for *The New York Times Magazine*, Ellery rented a set of studio portraits of stage stars who had played Hamlet in New York within living memory. Among them, as it happened, was a portrait of Van Harrison.

In The 45th Street Building Ellery prudently signed the after-hours check-in book in the elevator with the name "Barnaby Ross" and got off at the ninth floor. The sound of a vacuum cleaner led him to the propped-open door of a lighted office, and here he found a brawny-armed old woman in a tattered housedress with an apron over it.

"There's nobody here," she said, without looking up.

"Oh, yes, there is," said Ellery sternly. "There's you, and there's me, and it won't go any further if you come clean."

"Come what?" the cleaning woman straightened. "Don't you know you could go to jail for what you did, Mother?"

"I didn't do nothing!" she said excitedly. "What did I do?"

"You tell me." And Ellery thrust under her nose the portrait of Van Harrison.

The old woman paled. "He said nobody'd ever know …"

"There you are. You got them for him, didn't you?"

She looked him in the eye. "You a cop?"

Ellery sneered. "Do I look like a cop?"

"You won't tell the super?"

"I wouldn't give that screw the time of day."

"The man give me a big tip to keep my mouth shut …"

"I gather," said Ellery, removing a bill from his billfold, "that to open it again will require something larger."

"I'm a poor woman," said the old lady, eying the bill in Ellery's fingers, "and is that a twenty? The story is this: This good-looking gentleman comes up here one night after hours, like you, and he says to me he'll make it worth my while if I'll borry a few envelopes from some of the business offices on my floors, that's the eighth, ninth, and tenth. I says I can't do that, that's dishonest, and he says sure you can, what's dishonest about it, you heard of people who collect stamps and match-boxes and stuff, well I'm a collector of business envelopes, I go all over

54

the city making deals like this with cleaning women who can use an extra few bucks rather than bother busy business people and maybe get thrown out on my ear. So one thing leads to another, and I get him a stack of different envelopes from different firms on the three floors, and he gives me the tenspot and goes away, and I ain't laid eyes on him since. And that's the whole truth, Mister, so help me, and I hope you won't get me into no trouble with the super because I wasn't doing no harm, just a few lousy envelopes for a fruitcake. So now can I have that twenty?"

"The Dead End Kid, that's me," sighed Ellery; and he gave the old cleaning woman the bill, raised his hat, and went away.

The third letter came the following Wednesday. It was camouflaged in the envelope of a firm of accountants on the tenth floor of The 45th Street Building, the address on the envelope and the message on the sheet of plain white paper inside had again been typed with a red ribbon, and the message was:

Thursday, 8:30 P.M., C

This triumph of reasoning consoled Ellery until the following night, when he trailed Martha downtown on almost the identical route of ten days before. But this time her cab penetrated deeper south into The Bowery, passed the Canal Street entrance to Manhattan Bridge, and turned into the narrow Asiatic world of Mott Street.

It drew up at Number 45, and Martha disappeared in the Chinese Rathskeller.

So C stood for Chinatown and/or Chinese Rathskeller, and there was no longer any reason to doubt the orthodox sequence or application of the alphabet in Harrison's code.

It seemed like a meaty discovery until it was examined. On dissection it proved nutritious in appearance only. It advanced nothing.

Ellery felt sad as he went into the restaurant after an automatic interval and maneuvered himself to a table far enough away from Martha and Harrison to see without being seen. It all seemed so futile. What was he doing in Chinatown, spying on two people who were headed for the front pages of the tabloids? As he sourly consumed his *lot-fon-kare-ngow-yuk*—which had turned out to be beef, peppers, and tomatoes—he kept his eye on the lovers from a sense of duty only, conscious that he was not even aware of what he was being dutiful to.

And then he saw something that caused his gloomy ruminations to stop dead.

He had thought they were holding hands across the table. But when the waiter appeared with a trayful of steaming bowls, their hands parted company and Ellery saw that Harrison's had hold of something Martha's had slipped into it.

It was a small package, and the actor, after looking around, put it into his pocket.

D ...

"No, I don't,' said Ellery, steering Nikki around a mink coat holding a Scottie on a leash that was eying his leg thoughtfully. "It was done up in paper—in that lighting I couldn't get the color—and it was about three by *six*, and a half-inch or so thick."

"The booklet?" Nikki stopped to lean against the apartment house. It was a moonless night, and the river sounds were mournful. Everything floated tonight, people and sound and her thoughts.

"Wrong dimensions. What's the matter, Nikki?"

"Oh … I feel anesthetized. Swimming around in the ether. I keep forgetting what day it is."

"You're drugged with tension. Nikki, you can't keep on living like this. You'll break down. Why not give it up as a nice try?"

"No," said Nikki mechanically. She shook her head at a cigaret.

Ellery scowled as he lit one. He had never known this Nikki. She was as immovable as the wall she leaned against. He wondered what Martha would say—what depths of shame and remorse she might plumb—if she knew the heavy strength of Nikki's loyalty. But he knew he could never communicate such a thing to anyone in the world, especially to Martha. It had a mysterious, insoluble quality, like a faith, blind and so able to endure in darkness. And it occurred to him suddenly that Nikki had lost her mother very early and had never known a sister.

He sighed.

"You didn't spot anything roughly that size about the apartment, I suppose?"

"She wouldn't leave it lying around, Ellery."

"I'd have dismissed it as a meaningless gift, except that he looked around so peculiarly as he slipped it into his pocket. He was surreptitious about it. It wasn't in character. Or maybe it was. With a man of Harrison's type, you'd have to strip away a great many layers of hardened greasepaint before you got down to him … And Martha was relieved, it seemed to me. As if she'd found it a load to carry around. I don't understand it."

"Where did they go afterward?" asked Nikki dully. "She didn't get home till eleven-thirty."

"They didn't go anywhere. They left the Chinese Rathskeller about ten o'clock and simply drove around in a taxi until he dropped her off at Lexington and 42nd. She took another cab and went straight home. Where was she supposed to be tonight?"

"At the Music Hall catching the new Stanley Kramer picture to scout an unknown young actress she was tipped off about as a possible lead for the Greenspan play."

"That's taking a chance," muttered Ellery. "Suppose Dirk asks her about it? She's getting reckless."

"No," said Nikki. "Because Dirk doesn't know she saw the picture at a private showing two weeks ago."

"Oh," said Ellery.

Nikki said, "It's late, Ellery. I'd better be getting back upstairs."

They walked slowly along the pavement, and after a moment Ellery said, "About that booklet-"

"I've looked high and low for it, Ellery. I've gone through her night table, her secretary, her vanity, her bureau drawers, hatboxes, top shelf of her clothes closet—even the linen closet, the broom closet, and under her mattress. Wherever Dirk isn't apt to run across it. And … twice I went through her bag."

"Incredible!" exclaimed Ellery. "She must refer to it every time she gets a code message. Unless she's memorized all the code places, which doesn't seem likely. Have you thought of keeping an eye on her the mornings the letters come?"

"Of course, but I can hardly follow her into her bedroom when she's shut the door, Ellery. Or into the bathroom."

"No." And Ellery walked in silence. Then he said, "Nikki, I've got to get into the apartment."

Nikki stopped.

"It's got to be searched till the booklet is found. Knowing in advance where they're to meet at any given time may mean the difference between … well, it's obviously of the greatest importance. That code book's in the apartment somewhere—I can't see Martha running the risk of carrying it around with her. When is the next evening you're sure they'll both be out of the apartment at the same time?"

"This Saturday night. They're going to a party at the Boylands' in Scarsdale."

"There's no chance of a slip?"

"They're being picked up by Sarah and Jim Winegard—they're all driving up in Jim's car. That means they're more or less at the Winegards' mercy for transportation back. And you know Jim. He'll be the last one to leave."

"All right," said Ellery. "But let's play it smart. Tell them I'm coming up—if they don't mind—to clear out some manuscript correspondence with you on *EQMM*. Then nobody can accuse me of anything but slavedriving! … Good night."

"Good night, Ellery."

She looked so white and forlorn in the light of the entrance sidelamps that Ellery put his arms around her and kissed her in full view of the night doorman mopping down the lobby.

Ellery walked into the Lawrence apartment at five minutes after nine Saturday night, and at exactly nine-seven he found Martha's code book.

Nikki had admitted him to the apartment and left him in the living room while she stepped into the adjoining study to fetch her compact. She was just reaching for it in her bag beside the typewriter when Ellery appeared smiling in the doorway and holding aloft a paper-backed little book with a brightly colored laminated cover.

"Here it is," he said.

Nikki gaped as if he had been holding up the Gutenberg Bible.

Ellery went over to Dirk's green leather chair and settled himself with enjoyment. He began to leaf through the book.

"No," choked Nikki. "This is *too* much."

"What?" said Ellery. "Oh. Pooh. It was nothing at all."

"Oh, wasn't it," said Nikki fiercely. "Where did you find it? I've ransacked this apartment inside out, top to bottom, I don't know how many times!"

"Of course you did," said Ellery in a soothing voice, "and that's why you didn't find it. First principles, Nik. See Poe, Edgar Allan. Specifically *The Purloined Letter.*"

"An *obvious* place?"

"Right under your nose, sweetheart. It stood to reason that, if you couldn't find it in any of the hiding places you'd expect it to be, it must be in the one place nobody would dream of searching."

"But where?"

"Did you ever know a better place to hide a book than the average American bookcase?"

"On the living-room bookshelves," gasped Nikki.

"Sandwiched between a 1934 *World Almanac*," nodded Ellery, "and a copy of Darwin's *The Origin of Species*. In such company this little book could stand there undetected for three generations. Aren't you going to take a look at it?"

Nikki stalked over, head high, but craning. Ellery laughed and pulled her down, and after a moment she snuggled with a sigh into a comfortable position, and they looked the little book over together.

It was a guidebook by Carl Maas, *How to Know and Enjoy New York*, published in 1949 by the New American Library at thirty-five cents. The cover, which was illustrated by a photographic montage of Radio City, Times Square and New York Harbor, advertised its contents: "Where to Eat," "What to See," "How to Avoid the Clip Joints," and so on. It was written as a running account of the city's geography and places of interest, and one of its convenient features was that all place-names were printed in italic or in boldface type, making them stand out from the page.

Apparently Van Harrison had found this feature convenient, too, for here and there throughout the book certain place-names had been circled in red pencil, emphasizing them doubly.

"Confirms what we suspected," murmured Ellery. "I don't see a single duplication of places beginning with the same letter of the alphabet. It apparently runs once from *A* to *Z*. Let's check the *B* message. That 'Sammy's' of Sammy's Bowery Follies still bothers me."

"You passed it! Page nineteen."

"He put a red ring around 'Bowery Follies' and ignored the 'Sammy's' preceding it! So that's how Martha knew that was the *B*-place ..."

"Wait, Ellery. Here's Chinatown on the facing page, and it's not ringed–"

"I think I spotted it back here in the Foreign Restaurants section ... Yes, here, page eighty-six. Red ring around 'Chinese Rathskeller' and '45 Mott.' Thorough performer, isn't he? If he hadn't ringed the Chinatown address, too, she might have gone kiting off to the uptown branch on West 51st."

"Red," said Nikki. "Everything in red. I keep thinking of that darned scarlet letter."

"I'm tempted to say it's a manifestation of Harrison's sense of humor, but who knows? It may have a much simpler explanation. Tell you what you do, Nikki. Get over to the machine and type out this list as I give it to you. We'll forget *A*, *B*, and *C*–that's history. Make it *D* for whatever-it-is, and so on. I'll give you the page numbers, too. I may want to get a copy of the book for possible future developments."

"Carbon?"

"No. And I'll take the original with me. It's safer out of the apartment."

Ellery read the ringed items off as he came to them, page by page. When he had finished, Nikki made a second list, rearranging the items on the first sheet in alphabetical order. The original draft Ellery tore to shreds and flushed down the toilet.

"Now let's see what we have. Read them off, Nikki."

The list Nikki read contained twenty-three items, from *D* through *Z*:

D–(Billy Rose's) Diamond Horseshoe	on page 102
E–Empire State Building (102nd floor)	28
F–Fort Tryon Park (Cloisters)	49
G–Grant's Tomb	46
H–Hayden Planetarium	132
I–Idlewild	78
J–Jones Beach	123
K–Keen's (English) Chop House	82
L–Lewisohn Stadium	109
M–Macy's	28
N–New Madison Square Garden	31

"He's certainly playful," said Nikki wearily. "His mother must have been frightened by a sightseeing bus."

"It's probably a line he's worked out," said Ellery. "These great lovers are like the people who hang around the casinos. They've always got a system to beat the wheel. You can't deny it has its charm, Nikki."

"It escapes me."

"Well, it's apparently working on Martha. It adds a note of dash to the affair, no doubt. It's lucky he didn't have a copy of *The Third Man;* he'd have had her meeting him in a sewer." Ellery studied the list again. "I'm a lot more puzzled by something else."

"What now?" Nikki put her arms on the desk and her head on her arms.

"Well, their next meeting, for instance." Ellery glanced at her, but he went on as if he were concentrating on his thought. "*D.* Up to now they've met in pretty safe places—Chinatown, The Bowery; even their meeting at the A–wasn't dangerous the way they handled it. But the Diamond Horseshoe–a nightclub–in the heart of the theatrical district where they're both so well-known … It seems downright careless of Mr. Harrison. Any one of five hundred people might spot them there, and if it got back to Dirk … Are you all right, Nikki?"

"What?" Nikki looked up blearily.

Ellery went around the desk, put his hands under her arms, and lifted. "The meeting," he said firmly, "is adjourned."

"I'm all right, Ellery—"

"You're in the last stage of exhaustion. No, I'll put the book back before I leave." He carried her to her room, kicked the door open, and deposited her on the floor. "Get undressed."

"It's not even ten o'clock—"

"Do you undress yourself, or do I do it for you?"

Nikki sank wanly onto her makeshift bed. "You would pick a time when I'm half-dead." She yawned and shivered, hugging herself. "I suppose the next item on the agenda is to watch for the date and time of the Diamond Horseshoe meeting."

"Never mind that. I'm going to make you some hot milk, and then you're going to bed."

And the Diamond Horseshoe meeting was an interesting meeting, one point of interest being that it never took place.

Nikki phoned on Sunday morning to say that Martha and Dirk had come in at five A.M. from their Scarsdale party, making so much noise that the neighbors banged shoes on the walls. Nikki, lying awake in the dark, had heard Dirk yelling drunkenly in the kitchen that he would kill with his bare hands the next man she allowed to paw her, and Martha shrieking back that she couldn't stand it any more, nothing had happened in the world that any sane man could take exception to, and if he didn't stop assaulting men who danced with her and turning perfectly nice house parties into waterfront free-for-alls, with the police having to be called and everything—and a lucky thing for him Hal Boyland knew that state trooper personally!—why, so help her God, she would have him committed to a mental hospital; and so on, far into the morning. They had wound up hurling crockery at each other, which terminated hostilities, since an egg cup caught Dirk on the temple and opened a streaming cut over an inch long, at which Martha fainted and Nikki crawled out of bed to tend the wounded and clean the battlefield.

"I just looked in to see if they were dead or alive," sighed Nikki, "and Dirk's sleeping on the floor to one side of the bed and Martha's sleeping on the floor on the other side. I guess they had a last-gasp fight as to who would *not* sleep in the bed with whom, and couldn't settle even that. If it weren't so tragic it would be hilarious."

Sunday was passed in a truce of silence, with Nikki the desperate mediator. On Sunday night Dirk apologized, and Martha accepted his apology; and on Monday and Tuesday Dirk resumed his old, almost obsolete, canine habits and followed her wherever she went with humility and adoration. Martha was cool, but she stuck to home, and toward evening on Tuesday she thawed.

But on Wednesday morning the next letter came. *D* was the code designation, and the date and time were Friday at eight-fifteen P.M.

Ellery was at one of Mr. Rose's lonelier tables by seven-forty-five, hoping for an even break in the odds on Harrison's table being within range. He was studying the menu with both elbows elevated when Van Harrison walked in at seven-fifty-eight and was ushered to a reserved table of even lonelier location, with the odds going crazy. Harrison sat down not a dozen feet away. Fortunately again he was in profile to Ellery, and Ellery could watch him and the approach from the entrance at the same time.

Harrison ordered a cocktail.

Women were turning to look at him. He was dressed in a suede cream-gray suit with a white carnation in the lapel; diamonds glittered at his cuffs, and he raised and lowered his cocktail glass with a ceremoniousness that did his cufflinks full justice. His tempered profile he used like a rapier, keeping it carefully poised, or flicking it this way or that ever so slightly, with a half-smile on his lips, at once kind and masterful.

Didn't he know they were bound to be seen? Or didn't he care?

Ellery watched the women. They were impressed and delighted. He shook his head.

Then he realized that it was eight-twenty. Martha had not yet come. He wondered if his watch was right.

But he saw Harrison glancing at his wristwatch, too, with a frown.

Probably she was held up in traffic.

At eight-thirty-five Ellery began to doubt his traffic theory.

At eight-fifty he abandoned it.

At nine o'clock he knew Martha wasn't coming, and that was when he began to get the uneasy feeling that perhaps Dirk was.

Harrison was annoyed. Harrison was more than annoyed—he was livid. The table was set for two, and it was apparent to his public that the empty chair was going to remain empty. Some of the women were tittering.

At nine-five the actor summoned the maître and imperiously waved away the second chair and place-setting. His gestures and expression said that a stupid mistake had been made by the management. And a waiter ran up to take his food order.

He ordered coldly, in a loud voice.

Ellery rose and sought a phone.

The receiver at the other end was snatched up halfway through the first ring.

"Hello?" It was Martha's voice, dry, braced.

Before Ellery could answer he heard Dirk explode in the background. "Damn the phone! Hang up, Marty. The hell with whoever it is."

"But Dirk—Hello?"

"Ellery, Martha."

"Ellery. Hel*lo*, dear."

He wriggled at the relief in her voice.

"It's Ellery. How are you? Why haven't we seen you? Where are you calling from?"

Dirk's voice made some irritated sounds.

"I don't want to interrupt whatever you two are doing," Ellery said. "Is Nikki around?"

"Nikki, it's for you."

"I'll take it in the dressing room, Mar." Nikki, quick.

"Yes, do that!" Dirk.

"Dirk." Martha was laughing. "Don't mind him, Ellery. He's in one of his dedicated-artist moods. All *right*, Dirk! Why don't you drop in later, Ellery? He's really dying to see you. Me, too."

"Maybe I will. If I can get away, Martha."

"Here I am," panted Nikki. "Hang up, Mar! A girl has to have *some* privacy."

"Bye." Martha laughed; and he heard the click.

"Nikki?"

"Yes."

"Is it all right?"

"Yes. Dirk's got her occupied."

"What happened?"

"You at the—?"

"Yes."

"And the character—?"

"Still here, waiting. Dirk's doing?"

"Yes. He picked tonight to want to read his book to Martha as far as he's got. He's really terribly enthusiastic about it, so naturally—"

"Say no more. But wasn't she ready to go out?"

"Uh-huh. An appointment with a set designer ... she said. She phoned somebody with her back turned and left a message that Mrs. Lawrence couldn't make it at the last moment and would call tomorrow about another 'appointment.'"

"A message he didn't get. Okay, Nik. I was worried."

"What are you going to do?"

"Hang around here a while. Maybe I'll drop in later."

"Oh, do!"

Ellery went back to his table.

Something new had been added during his absence. A thin small man in a dinner jacket had his palms planted on Van Harrison's table and was leaning over it, talking. The man had pointed ears and a Hallowe'en smile and whatever he was saying amused him greatly. But it was not amusing Van Harrison. Harrison was looking ugly and old. His long, beautiful hands were clasped about his soup bowl and his knuckles showed pale points. Ellery had the oddest conviction that what Van Harrison wanted to do, more than anything else in the world at that moment, was to pick up the bowl and jam it over the thin man's face.

Then the man in the dinner jacket turned his head slightly and Ellery recognized him. It was Leon Fields.

Fields's syndicated column, *Low and Inside*, was the *pièce de résistance* of over six hundred daily newspapers serving the appetites for gossip, rumor, and innuendo of unestimated millions of the sensation-hungry. His juiciest paragraphs were headed: LEON FIELDS MEAN TODAY, and these dished out the *filets mignons* of his nightly shopping excursions in the supermarkets of Broadway and café society. As a famous wit remarked to Ellery one night at the Colony, while they watched Fields tablehopping, "One hint that Leon's in the neighborhood, and nobody goes to bed."

66

Fields had the unadmired reputation of never losing his meat once he got the scent. On the Rialto it was earnestly said that nothing had been surer than death and taxes until Leon Fields came along.

Ellery had followed his career with clinical interest, and it had only recently dawned on him that Fields was a much-maligned character. The evidence was hidden and scattered, but it was there. Viewed without prejudice, Fields's activities took on an almost moral blush. He never hounded the innocent; his victims were invariably guilty. Unsavory as some of his tidbits were, no one had ever been able to make him swallow his own words. When Fields printed it, there was a fact behind it somewhere. And Ellery had heard of numerous targets of other columnists whom Fields had spared because they were victims of circumstances. He was as quick to defend as to condemn, and some of his most vicious manhunts had been undertaken in the interests of the helpless and the wronged. He had once written in his column: "Last week a Certain Nobody called me a son-of-a-you-know. Thanks, pal. *My* mother was an underdog. What was yours?"

The possibility that Leon Fields was on the trail of Van Harrison lowered Ellery's body-temperature with great rapidity.

He watched anxiously.

And suddenly Harrison was on his feet, fists waving. He said something to Fields, and the thin man's smile vanished. The columnist's hand reached for the sugar bowl. Harrison began to shove the table aside.

The floor-show was on and all eyes were on the performers. No one seemed to notice what was happening.

Ellery looked around. He could not afford to be seen by Harrison. But unless he could avert a brawl …

"Quick!" He grabbed the sleeve of the passing maître. "Break that up if you don't want trouble!"

The startled maître got there just as Van Harrison's arm came up with a fist at the end of it. He caught the fist, stepped between the two men, and said something very quickly. A large man in a tuxedo appeared from nowhere. In a moment the group had left the floor and two waiters were clearing Harrison's table.

Ellery shoved a ten-dollar bill into his waiter's hand and hurried after them.

They were in a milling huddle at the checkroom, Harrison being held ungently by the large man in the tuxedo. Ellery walked up behind Harrison and handed the girl his check and a quarter.

"Let go of me," he heard Harrison say in a strangled baritone. "Take your hands off me."

"Let him go," said the columnist. "He's harmless."

"Okay if you say so, Mr. Fields," said the large man.

"Just let me pay my check," the actor raged. "If you're not a yellow dog, you'll be waiting for me outside."

Fields spun on his heel and walked out.

A crowd was gathering. The large man began to disperse them.

Harrison flung a bill at the headwaiter, jammed his Homburg on his head, and strode out. His cheeks were gray and they were quivering.

Ellery followed.

The sidewalk under the marquees was deserted; plays along 46th Street had just settled down to their second acts. The columnist was waiting under the marquee of a darkened theater ten yards up the street.

Harrison broke into a run. Toward Fields.

Ellery quickened his pace, looking back over his shoulder. A knot of people had formed at the entrance of the Diamond Horseshoe, craning. As he looked, they began to move toward him in a body. Somebody across the street turned to shout something. A man wearing a camera on a leather strap appeared, stared, began to cross on a long diagonal run. A cruising cab shot by, jammed on its brakes, and backed up to the dark theater.

When Ellery turned around, Harrison and Fields had disappeared.

He lowered his head and sprinted.

"They're in the alley." The cab driver was leaning out. "What is it, a fight?"

"For God's sake, don't go away!" Ellery dashed into the alley.

They were rolling up and down in the darkness. The actor was cursing and sobbing, Fields was silent. He's slighter and shorter than Harrison, thought Ellery, and thirty pounds lighter. He hasn't a chance.

Ellery groped toward the commotion, shouting, "Stop it, you fools! Do you want the police in on this?"

A tangle of arms and legs jarred him, and he staggered back to bang his shoulder blades against the brick wall of the theater.

Something flashed at the head of the alley and his arm instinctively came up to protect his face. The man with the camera ... There was a crowd on the sidewalk, blocking the exit. Then the darkness fell again, darker than before.

Suddenly he heard Leon Fields cry out. There was a scrambling sound, and all sound stopped.

"Where are you, damn it!" Ellery snarled. "What did you do to him?"

Harrison stumbled by, still cursing. The camera flashed again. The actor lowered his head like a bull, charged, and scattered the crowd.

A woman screamed, "Don't let him get away!"

A man jeered, "Okay, lady. You stop him."

Nobody came into the alley but the cameraman. Ellery heard him swearing; he had dropped his case of bulbs.

Ellery found Fields lying face down on the cement, unconscious. He felt swiftly for blood, but could locate none. He slung the little columnist over his shoulder and lumbered up the alley, keeping his head down.

"It's all right," he kept saying. "One side, please. Just a brawl ... Cab!"

The last thing Ellery heard as the taxi shot away from the curb was the cameraman, still swearing.

"Who was that other guy, Gorgeous George?" asked the cab driver. "Is he still out?"

"He's coming to now."

"Too bad it was dark in the alley. I bet it was a pip. Where to, bud?"

"Just get out of Times Square."

Leon Fields groaned. Ellery chafed his hands, slapped his cheeks.

He was thinking: Dirk doesn't know what he accomplished tonight. If Martha had been there ... He could see the tabloids clearly, and he shut his eyes. As it was, the story would break with a roar. ACTOR SLUGS FIELDS. With action pictures ...

Fields said: "Who the hell are you?"

"Your fairy godmother," said Ellery. "How's your jaw?"

"Fields feels lousy." The columnist tried to peer through a rapidly swelling eye. "Say, I know you. You're Inspector Q's little boy. Did you rescue me from the bad man?"

69

"I picked up the remains."

"He fights dirty. Gave me the knee and when I doubled up beat the hell out of my face. Am I dreaming, or did somebody take pictures?"

"You're awake."

"Who was it?"

"Some news photographer on roving assignment, I think."

"Great," growled Fields. "What they'll do to this." He was silent, then he said, "What's your hatchet?"

"No hatchet."

"I'll bet."

"You'd lose."

Fields grunted. "Anyway, thanks."

"Don't mention it."

"Know who he was?"

"Yes."

"Who?" Fields peered again.

"V.H."

"Give me a cigaret. I seem to have lost mine in the scuffle."

He smoked silently, thinking. His jaw was swollen as well as his eyes; he smoked sidewise, wryly. His dinner clothes were a mess.

"Look, my friends," said the voice from the driver's seat, "I don't mind cruising around on the clock, but would you at least give me a clue where I'm going to wind up?"

Fields said in a swift undertone, "Does he know who—?"

"I don't believe so."

"Don't tell him. I want to play this coy tonight. I've got to clear my head. Can I trust you?"

"How should I know what you can do?"

"Okay. Tell him Park and 86th. Where are we now?"

"Third Avenue around 60th, I think."

"Tell him."

Ellery told the driver and dropped his voice still lower. "What's the idea? Don't you live at Essex House?"

"That's for my public. I've got a few hideouts around town under different names. I don't think I'm up to answering my phone tonight. Where I'm going, the calls are from hipsters."

"Just what did you say to our friend," asked Ellery with innocent curiosity, "that aroused his ire?"

The columnist grinned.

They got out at Park and 86th and stood on the corner until the taxi was out of sight.

"Now where?" asked Ellery.

"You're sticking, I see."

"I don't give a damn where you hole up. You need first aid."

Fields stared at him out of his one usable eye. Suddenly he said, "All right."

They walked up Park Avenue to 88th Street and turned west. At Madison they crossed over.

"It's this one here."

It was a small, quiet-looking apartment house between Madison and Fifth. Fields unlocked the street door and they went in. The elevator was self-service; there was no doorman.

He led the way to a rear apartment on the ground floor, used his key again. The name panel over the bell button said: GEORGE T. JOHNSON.

"I like ground-floor apartments," Fields said. "You can jump out of a window in an emergency."

The flat was furnished in surprisingly good taste. The columnist saw Ellery looking around, and he laughed. "Everybody thinks I'm a slob. But even a slob can have a soul, hm? If I told any of the wolf pack that I'm queer for Bach, they'd turn pale. I'll tell you a secret—I can't stand boogy. Makes my stomach turn over. What do you drink?"

They had a couple of quick ones and then Ellery went to work on him. An hour later, bathed, cuts cleansed, swellings down, and in pajamas and robe, Fields looked human again.

They had a couple of slow ones.

"I don't drink when I'm working," said the columnist, "but you're company."

"I don't, either," said Ellery, "so I'm breaking my rule."

Fields pretended not to understand. He talked charmingly on a dozen subjects as he kept refilling Ellery's glass.

"It won't do you any good," said Ellery an hour later, "because while most times three drinks can put me under, I have a hollow leg when

I put my mind to it. Well, maybe not quite–that sounded like a mixed metaphor. The point is, Leon, how come?"

"How come what?"

"How come you know what."

"Let's have some Bach."

Ellery listened to Landowska's brittle beauties for another hour. Under other circumstances he would have enjoyed it. But his head was beginning to dance and Fields's battered face was dancing with it. He yawned.

"Sleepy?" said the columnist. "Have another." He turned off the record player and came on with the bottle.

"Enough," said Ellery.

"Aw, come on."

"More than enough," said Ellery. "What are you trying to do to me?"

The columnist grinned. "What you wanted to do to me. Tell me, Ellery: What tomahawk are you polishing?"

"Let's call it a draw. Are you feeling all right?"

"Sure."

"I'm going home."

Fields took him to the door. "Just tell me this: Are you working on Van Harrison?"

Ellery looked at him. "Why should I be working on Van Harrison?"

"Who's asking?"

"Who's telling?"

They collapsed in each other's arms, overcome by their wit. Then Fields put his arm around Ellery and said, "You're okay, chum. So you've got something on that bastard. Maybe I know it and maybe I don't–"

"Maybe you're talking through your father's mustache, Leon."

"Let's stop horsing around." The columnist's chopped-up face was grim. "If I gave you some of the dirt I've got stashed away on Harrison, would it help you?"

Ellery took a long time before he answered. Then he said: "Maybe."

"Okay, I'll think about it."

They embraced again, and Ellery staggered out into the night.

E·F·G·

Ellery crawled out of bed on Saturday morning to find that it was almost noon and that the life of a private eye was composed of lows as well as highs. His head felt rotten clear through and he bore it gingerly from the bathroom to the kitchen. Here he found the morning newspapers neatly waiting. On the top one, the *Daily News*, his father had drawn an arrow in red crayon over the figure of a man in a full front-page photo, and he had scrawled above it: "Is this resemblance coincidental, or are you the copyright owner?"

It was the flash photo of himself slammed against the wall of the alley, with Harrison and Fields locked in combat at his feet.

Ellery poured himself a cup of bitter coffee from the pot thickening on the range, and he sat down at the kitchen table to survey the damage.

The Inspector's identification of him had been compounded of equal parts of guesswork and inside information. Nikki might do as well, but he doubted if anyone else would recognize him. The photograph was all right. His arm had come up just in time to black out the salient parts of his face. Of the two men rolling on the floor of the alley, only Leon Fields's face was visible, but it was grotesquely twisted with pain from a blow and was hardly recognizable. Harrison sprawled above him, his face turned from the camera. The story on page three was illustrated with the photo of Harrison charging up the alley in his getaway, but even this head-on shot showed the head lowered in distorting perspective. Apparently neither photograph had been clear, for both had been hastily retouched, causing further distortion. They would make little visual impression on the public.

The story was sparse. Both combatants were named in the headlines, and the time and place were stated in the boldface type of the lead paragraph, but the man who had made off with the unconscious Fields was "unidentified" and was referred to, simply, as "the Mystery Man." Mystery Man was being sought by the police, as was the driver of the taxi. Columnist Leon Fields had not been located for a statement; by press time he had not appeared at his home or any of his known haunts, and a spot-check of the hospitals had failed to turn him up. "Fields may be hiding out with friends." Van Harrison's telephone in Darien, Connecticut, did not answer; he had not gone to the Lambs Club: "The police are checking the midtown hotels."

The cause of the fist fight was unknown. "A quick run-through of Fields's recent columns shows no reference to Actor Van Harrison, good or bad. Harriet Loughman, Fields's Girl Friday, refused comment, saying 'Any statement will have to come from Mr. Fields.'"

The other newspapers carried terse news accounts of the fracas. None had any pictures, and none front-paged the story.

Ellery went into his father's bedroom with his coffee cup and the copy of the *News* and used the Inspector's direct line to Headquarters.

"I've been waiting for your call," said Inspector Queen's acid tones. "What happened last night?"

"Who's speaking, please?"

"Your old man," said his old man, sweetening.

"Then I'll tell you." And Ellery gave his father an account of the previous night's events. "I haven't seen the afternoon papers. What's the latest?"

"Fields came out of hiding and issued a statement to the effect that 'it's a tempest in a cocktail shaker.' He claims he stopped by Harrison's table, Harrison was a little tight and misunderstood something he, Fields, said; that Harrison then challenged Fields to 'come outside,' adding a number of uncomplimentary remarks; that he, Fields, thereupon lost his temper and indicated his willingness to oblige, in the great American tradition; and so forth. He refused to say what it was that Harrison 'misunderstood,' and he said he had no idea who the man was who put him in a cab. 'Just a Good Samaritan,' he said. 'I told him where to take me, he did it, I thanked him, and that's the last I saw of him.' Asked if he'd recognize the Good Samaritan if he saw him again, Fields said, 'I doubt it. I wasn't seeing very good at the time.' Why's he protecting *you*?"

74

"I don't know," said Ellery thoughtfully, "unless he's so anxious to see Harrison take a pratfall he doesn't want to hamstring me in whatever it is he thinks I'm up to. Did they find Harrison? He wasn't fished out of the river, or anything?"

"No such luck," said his father. "He rolled up to his house in Darien around five-thirty A.M. in his brand-new Caddy convertible and walked right into the arms of the reporters, who'd broken in and'd been waiting there all night lapping up his liquor and trying on his toupees."

"Toupees?" Ellery was startled. "You mean that isn't his own hair?"

"He owns only about fifty per cent of it, I'm told. He also wears a corset. They found two spares in his bureau."

"Heavens to Betsy."

"In fact, if they'd found a set of store teeth and a bullet hole between his eyes I'd think we were back in the Elwell case."

"I wonder if these personality sidelights," mused Ellery, "are known to a certain …"

"Would depend, I should think," said the Inspector sedately. "Women aren't as disillusioned by these things as men, anyway. Do you want his statement, or don't you?"

"His statement. To be sure."

"It was pretty much along the lines of Leon's, except that Harrison said it was Fields who was plastered. He wouldn't let on what the fight was about, either. Dismissed it as a mere nothing—'an alcoholic afflatus,' as he put it. After he got away from the alley, he went on to say, he picked up his car at an all-night parking lot and drove around for hours 'cooling off.' He probably spent the night in some Westchester bar, because he was thoroughly fried when he got home. He expressed his regrets at having lost his temper and 'hoped' he hadn't roughed up Mr. Fields too much. In fact, Harrison got quite expansive with the boys. Practically had them feeling his muscle. There was a bad moment when one of the reporters was so indelicate as to suggest that maybe the weight and reach differential had something to do with his glorious victory, and it almost wound up in another brawl. But in the end Harrison said he'd be only too happy to pay for any medical expenses Mr. Fields may have had to incur, and apologize to boot."

"Worrying about an assault rap," chuckled Ellery. "I take it Leon isn't pressing a charge."

"That's right. So that's the end of the Battle of the Alley."

"Just one other thing, Dad. Did either man, or any of the news stories or off-the-record remarks, even hint at a possible woman in the case?"

"As far as I know, no."

"Thank you," said Ellery fervently; and he hung up just as the door buzzed.

It was Nikki. She rushed in crying, "Ellery! What happened?"

So Ellery soothed her and made her comfortable in the study while he retired to dress, and through the door of his bedroom repeated once more the saga of the previous night.

At the end Nikki said slowly, "I wonder if it wasn't about Martha."

"I don't think so. I don't see Fields hushing up a noisy yarn like that. It's the sort of thing that's–if he'll pardon the expression–right up his alley. No, Nikki, it was something else, and I'd give a great deal to know what."

"Why?"

"Because whatever it is, you can bank on it it's not to Harrison's credit. Leon deals in well-hung beef, with an odor. If we knew what it was, it might come in awfully handy … But tell me about Martha," Ellery said, appearing in the doorway knotting his tie. "How did she take it? What did Dirk say?"

"She put on a marvelous act. But she almost overdid it, looking so blank at Harrison's name in the paper that Dirk had to remind her she'd met him 'once.' She pretended such indifference that I thought Dirk gave her a queer look." Nikki shuddered. "She must be in torture, Ellery. She doesn't dare try to call Harrison, and she must be scared witless that he'll try to call her. I noticed she kept within arm's length of the phone all morning."

"Didn't Dirk make any comment?"

"Only that if Leon Fields had something on Harrison, he wouldn't be in Harrison's shoes for all the empty seats on Broadway."

"How right he is. Well, you'd better keep your eye peeled for the next business envelope. Martha may beat you to it."

This was a prophecy. On Monday morning Nikki hurried out of her room at the usual time, bound for the lobby and the mail, to find that Martha had already been downstairs for it and was shuffling the envelopes rapidly.

"Aren't you the early one this morning?" Nikki said brightly. She tried desperately to keep up with the envelopes, on the lookout for the telltale red typing.

Martha smiled and dropped the letters on the foyer table. "The usual nothing," she said indifferently. "I'll look at them later. The coffee's making, Nikki …"

On Tuesday morning she did the same thing.

"I don't know what we'll do if she keeps this up," Nikki said over the phone Tuesday evening. "If she gets to it first, I'll never see it."

"Illustrating the futility of this whole damn thing," growled Ellery. "What's the point, Nikki? So I follow them through the alphabet and back again—and then what? I've been trying to do some work of my own, and this day- and nightmare is making it impossible."

"I'm sorry," said Nikki frigidly. "Of course you mustn't let your work suffer. Why don't you hire a secretary?"

"I've got a secretary!"

"No, I mean it, Ellery. Forget the whole thing. It *is* an imposition—"

"Imposition my foot. It's a stupidity. I'd be far better off following Dirk. Less wear and tear, and surer results. That is, if the object is to keep him from knocking their heads together. *Is* that the object? I don't know up from down any more."

"I want this affair stopped," Nikki whispered. "As well as kept from Dirk. Harrison's not right for Martha, Ellery. He's no good. I've—I've asked around. Some way has to be found to bring her to her senses, and it has to be done before Dirk finds out. Maybe you'll see an opportunity to break it up—somehow, some night, when they meet. Don't you see, Ellery?"

"I see," sighed Ellery; and in the end he agreed to trail Martha blindly on whichever days Nikki was unable to get to the mail first.

Happily for Ellery, Martha as well as Van Harrison had been thoroughly frightened by the Fields affair. Not only did Harrison refrain from sending a message for two weeks afterward, but Martha clung to hearth and husband as if they were the most desirable things in life. What those two weeks meant to her, Ellery could only imagine from Nikki's eye-witness reports. She was evidently afraid to leave the premises, since Harrison might rashly phone, as he had done before the first letter came; at the same time she must have had to fight night and day the temptation to slip out and phone him. The result was a suspension in time; and it made of Martha a pitiful ghost, drifting about the apartment with an eager-to-please smile which she put on and took off like her bedroom slippers. Dirk seemed puzzled; he kept asking her if anything was the matter. She would murmur something about having to wait while Ella Greenspan rewrote her second act, and steal away to her bedroom at the first opportunity, as if it were too dangerous to remain under Dirk's eye another moment.

What Harrison was waiting for was evidently the disappearance of *l'affaire* Alley from the newspapers. When four days passed without reference to it, the fifth letter suddenly came.

They were lucky. Martha had got the mail first, as usual, but Nikki caught a glimpse of a buff-colored business envelope with the address typed in red as Martha went into the bathroom and locked the door.

"Just try to let me know when she's getting ready to leave the apartment," Ellery said when Nikki phoned him at noon that day. "The appointment is probably for tomorrow. But don't take any chances."

The next morning Martha left the apartment at ten o'clock to drop in on Ella Greenspan, she said, and see how her author was coming along with the script. Nikki phoned Ellery as Martha was putting her hat on. They had a short conversation about a mislaid non-existent book of Nikki's. The moment she hung up, Ellery left.

But he was too late. When he stepped out onto the observation terrace on the 102nd floor of the Empire State Building, there was no sign of either Harrison or Martha. He waited a few minutes in the lounge, and then he sought an attendant. He was careful to describe only Harrison.

"Yes, sir, the gentleman was here about fifteen minutes ago. I remember because he was joined by a lady and instead of going out to look at the view they took the elevator right down again."

So Ellery went back home, shrugging all the way.

78

Nikki's subsequent report was curious. Dirk had been reminiscently fretful from the moment the door shut on Martha. He had taken to pacing and muttering to himself while he eyed the telephone. Finally, at eleven o'clock, he had seized the Manhattan telephone book, looked up a number, and dialed.

"Mrs. Greenspan? This is Dirk Lawrence. Is my wife there?"

And Martha had been there! Dirk's mood lightened by magic. They had an idiotic conversation and he hung up in high spirits to resume dictating.

"Cute," remarked Ellery. "She knew he'd be suspicious when she left the house alone for the first time in a couple of weeks. She and Harrison must have had all of five precious minutes together. I wonder what they found to talk about."

"I don't care," said Nikki happily. "We've passed *E.*"

"You sound like the editor of a dictionary project," snapped Ellery. "Let me know when you get to *F.*"

They got to *F* five days later. This time Nikki had no difficulty intercepting the letter. Martha, she said, had stopped getting up early.

"Fort Try on Park—The Cloisters—at one P.M. tomorrow."

Ellery's car was laid up with carburetor trouble, and he decided on the 8th Avenue subway as the least painful way of reaching Manhattan's far north. He got off at the 190th Street-Overlook Terrace station.

It lacked a few minutes of one o'clock; The Cloisters did not open to the public until one. Ellery approached the towered building cautiously. He was just in time to see Martha step from a taxi into a red Cadillac convertible and the convertible shoot away.

"I keep forgetting," Ellery told Nikki that night, "that they're not really interested in sightseeing. Harrison's guidebook refers to points of contact only. I'm sorry, Nikki. Shadowing doesn't seem to be my forte."

"I don't suppose it matters." Nikki was very nervous tonight; she kept lighting cigarets and putting them down. "I saw something this evening that I don't think I ever want to see again."

"What's happened now?"

"She was away all afternoon. Dirk was very upset. He dictated hardly a line. I didn't hear what alibi she prepared for herself, but what-

79

ever it was it didn't satisfy him. He kept making calls to various places where she might be, and of course he didn't get her or turn up anyone who'd seen her. When she came home ... I think," Nikki said, "I need a drink."

Ellery gave her straight Scotch. She took the glass, but then she put it down. "No, that's what *he* did. It doesn't solve a thing ... He jumped on Martha before she could peel her gloves off. Where had she been, what man had she been with this time–he had the goods on her–she hadn't been where she'd said she was going–now he knew he'd been right all along ... You can imagine.

"Or rather," said Nikki, staring into the recent past, "you can't. Dirk can be the sweetest guy in the world one minute and the most loathsome the next. He has a foul tongue when he gets these attacks, Ellery, and I mean foul. Some of the things he said to Martha tonight–if any man said them to me, husband or no husband, I'd kill him."

"But if they were true?" said Ellery.

"They couldn't be true. Even if she's doing all the unspeakable things he accuses her of, they're not true the way he means them. Martha isn't a whore, Ellery. Whatever she's doing with Van Harrison, it's because she thinks she's in love with him. That makes the difference. Maybe no man can see that it would, but it does ... And then," said Nikki, a great many decibels lower, "Dirk beat her."

"*Beat* her?"

"He hit her a tremendous blow on the side of the head and she fell down. Her earlobe started to bleed; she was dazed and tried to get up. He hit her again ... with his fist this time. And this time she stayed down. She–she didn't make a sound. Didn't cry out, or whimper, or anything. She just took it. As if her tongue had been cut out. As if she was afraid that if she made the slightest sound, he'd kill her."

Nikki started to cry. "You can't imagine how awful he looked," she wailed. "You can't imagine. His face was the face of a maniac. I was so frightened. I thought of the gun in his bureau drawer, and I kept saying to myself that if he hit her once more I'd snatch it out and shoot him. But he ran into the study and slammed the door ...

"I wanted to phone you right away, but I had to take care of Martha. I bathed her face and head and undressed her and got her into bed, and all the time she didn't say a word, Ellery. And I didn't know what to say, either ... It wasn't till I gave her a sleeping pill that she said–do you know what she said, Ellery?"

"What did she say?"

" 'Lock me in, Nikki.' "

Ellery wiped her face and sat down and took her hand. "I locked her in, and I pocketed the key. Then I went to the study. I don't know what I was going to do ... But I found him stretched out in the armchair, dead to the world. He'd swallowed most of a fifth of Scotch in about fifteen minutes. So I locked him in, too. And I grabbed a cab and came over here, and now I've got to get back. Maybe he'll be sick and wake up, or something ..."

"I'm going back with you," said Ellery grimly.

But the Lawrence apartment was quiet. Martha was sleeping heavily in the bedroom. Dirk was where Nikki had left him, snoring in drunken sleep.

"You go to bed, Nikki. I think you'd better sleep with Martha. And just to be on the safe side, keep the door locked."

Nikki clung to him. "Ellery, I wish you didn't have to leave."

"I'm not going to leave."

"What are you going to do?" Nikki whispered.

"Stick with Dirk till he comes to. Till I can find out how far this has gone in his so-called mind."

He kissed her and waited until he heard the key turn in the bedroom door.

Then he went back to the study.

Dirk awoke at dawn. He gave a strangled snort, and Ellery heard the creak of the armchair springs.

Ellery got off the living-room couch and went to the doorway between the two rooms. Dirk was swaying on his feet in the half-light, hands to his cheeks, shaking his head as if he had water in his ears.

"No," said Ellery, "you didn't dream it."

Dirk's face came out of his hands like an explosion. His body contracted in a curve.

"Nerves, old man?"

"What are you doing here?" Dirk's voice was a croak.

"Oh, come on, you can write better dialogue than that. What do you suppose I'm doing here? I left a perfectly good secretary on deposit. I didn't expect to get back a screaming hysteric."

"She told you about it." Dirk dropped into the chair.

"Did you think she'd keep it a secret? You scared the wadding out of her, Dirk. I came back to protect her, since for some unimaginable reason she refuses to leave. But that doesn't settle the question of Martha."

Dirk got up again. "Where is she?"

"Suppose I told you she's on a slab at the Morgue."

"Look, Ellery, I'm in no condition for jokes."

"Suppose I told you it isn't a joke."

Dirk's jaw wigwagged before anything came out. "You mean I—you mean she—"

"Suppose I told you that second sock to her head broke her neck."

Dirk laughed. He went over to the desk and picked up the bottle of Scotch. He held it up critically to the brightening light. "You sonofabitch," he said. "You had me going. It wasn't her head I hit the second time. It was her shoulder." He drained the bottle. It dropped from his fingers and he collapsed in the armchair and covered his face again. "How is she?"

"Last I saw, she was sleeping." Dirk began to get up. "Relax. Nikki's sleeping with her, and she locked the door. At Martha's request." Dirk sank back again. "How do you like it, champ? Proud of yourself?" Ellery came in and picked up the empty bottle and looked at it. "Is there anything more pitiful—and useless—than morning-after remorse? You don't even have the satisfaction of knowing that you beat her up drunk."

Dirk said nothing.

"Dirk." Ellery placed the bottle carefully on the desk. "What's this all about?"

"I told you!"

"Do you expect me to believe you can't control these emotional binges?"

"I don't expect you to believe anything. Let me alone."

"It's not safe. You're getting dangerous."

"All right, I know, I'm sorry, I'll crawl on my navel," said Dirk bitterly. "But this time it wasn't my imagination. She's seeing somebody, Ellery."

"Any proof of that?" Ellery asked crisply.

"Not your kind, no. But she got careless yesterday. For the first time she didn't bother to go where she'd said she was going. She forgot to cover herself." Dirk jumped up and began to stride about. "I don't make out a good case. I lose control and rage and throw my weight around. Okay, I'm all wrapped up in myself and nobody loves a breast-beater–or a wife-beater–and Martha's pink and sweet and has a soft voice and I'm seeing things. But suppose I'm not! Suppose she isn't what everybody thinks she is … what I thought she was when I married her. Then what?"

"Then," said Ellery, "if you can prove it, you say: Sorry, my error; and you bow out."

"Is that what you'd do if your wife was sleeping with another man?"

"It's your wife we're discussing. And if she is, you don't know it. And even if she is–how clean is your nose?"

"What do you mean?" Dirk looked ugly. "I haven't given the time of day to another woman since I met Martha!"

"Pull your jaw back in. I'm willing to take your word for it. But a husband's catting around isn't the only reason a wife gets itchy feet. Maybe you've accused Martha so often of being unfaithful when she wasn't that she's decided she might as well be."

Dirk looked trapped.

"It's probably still not too late, Dirk. Maybe she is seeing another man, but that doesn't mean she's gone the limit. She's still in love with you or she'd have walked out on you long ago. If I were you, I'd have another go at a good analyst and meanwhile I'd try my damnedest to save what's left of my marriage. You're not going to do it with your fists."

To himself Ellery said, And may God have mercy on my soul.

He left Dirk staring at the wall and shut the study door quietly. And there was Nikki, her red hair tumbled about her face, clutching her robe at the throat.

Ellery took her into the foyer. "You look very pretty in the morning."

Nikki looked bewildered.

"Martha still asleep?"

"Yes," Nikki whispered.

"I think this crisis is past. But it can't go on much longer. I'm going to have to talk to Martha."

83

"Here?"

"Hardly."

"I don't think she'll talk to you, Ellery. She's so far committed ... and especially after last night ..."

"She's going to come to me."

"She won't."

"She will. At her next meeting she'll catch a glimpse of me. She'll be scared. She'll come, all right ... In that kind of climate, I have a fighting chance to talk some sense into her." Ellery added slowly, "It may be our last chance."

The following week Nikki tipped Ellery off that the G letter had arrived.

"How's it been going, Nikki?"

"All right. Martha hasn't been able to go out because of her face. At first she wouldn't talk to him, and he's been quiet as a mouse. But he's tried to make up to her in his own way. He sent her a box of gardenias yesterday. They're her favorite flowers. That did it. Women are such fools!"

"Do you think she'll keep the appointment?"

"I don't know. The swelling's down ... I suppose so."

"Don't bother phoning me when she leaves. I'll just chance it. The worst that can happen is that I'll have a visit with General Grant."

Harrison had set the time for two in the afternoon of the next day. It was a fine day, and Ellery walked over to Riverside Drive, striding.

But the nurses were out with their baby carriages, and assorted children, many children, were playing on the grass overlooking the West Side Highway and the Hudson. Two women were clucking over a red-faced lump in a carriage, the lump evidently being one of the newly made ones.

Ellery scowled at the little products of love. The day wasn't so fine after all. He found himself wishing he were on the trail of a nice, clean murder.

He took a bus the rest of the way.

He got off at 122nd Street and crossed over from the Riverside Church to the paved plaza before Grant's Tomb. The plaza, the steps were deserted. He looked at his watch. Five minutes of two.

He went in boldly, hoping to surprise them. But the Tomb was empty, too.

The marble floor sent his footsteps echoing through the building. He leaned on the railing and looked down at the historic remains a dozen feet below. Ulysses Simpson Grant had been lying here since 1897, and he had been dead fifteen years before that. Julia Dent Grant's tenure was newer, but still fifty years old. You're dead a long time, Ellery thought, and nobody much cares. I'll have to bring Dirk here for a lesson in historical perspective.

He heard a car horn outside and he went quickly out of the Tomb. He stopped between two of the pillars above the stone steps, shading his eyes against the glare.

The red convertible was at the curb of the plaza. Van Harrison's Homburg and broad back were visible at the wheel. He was honking at a cab parked on the east side of the Drive. As Ellery glanced over, the cab drove away. It unveiled Martha, on the sidewalk.

She had to wait for the traffic signal. She was dressed gaily today, in something flowered, with bright colors, and a big picture hat. She was holding the floppy brim against the breeze with one hand and waving with the other.

Ellery stepped out of the shadows of the pillars and onto the apron of the stairs, and he deliberately waved back.

She spotted him instantly. Her hand stopped flapping; she half-turned, as if to run.

Harrison honked again, surprised. Then he turned his head.

Ellery ran down the steps, waving cheerfully. "Hi, Martha!"

She changed her mind and came hurrying across the Drive, clutching her hat. Now that the die was cast, she was trying to beat him to the convertible.

Ellery allowed her to get there first. But he came on quickly enough to immobilize them.

Harrison had jumped out and was saying something to her in a swift undertone. He turned, smiling, as Ellery came up.

"Why, Ellery." Martha was smiling, too. She was very pale. "I've never pictured you visiting tombs, except on a case."

"There are all sorts of cases." Ellery glanced at the actor in the expectant manner of one waiting to be introduced.

"Oh. This is Van Harrison. Ellery Queen."

"How d'you do." Harrison squeezed, hard.

"Strong handshake, Mr. Harrison," said Ellery, waving his fingers. "Impressive. Well, I don't want to hold you up, Martha. Happy to have met you, Mr. Harrison—"

"I wanted to talk to Mr. Harrison about a part," said Martha pathetically. "In the play I'm doing this fall. He was kind enough to meet me—"

"Of course, Martha. See you!"

"Can I drop you off somewhere?" asked the actor, still smiling.

"No, no, don't bother. I'd only be in the way." Ellery walked off, waving.

When he looked back, the convertible was gone.

She pressed the buzzer of the Queen apartment before ten the following morning.

"Come in, Martha," said Ellery soberly.

She was hatless, in a housedress. It was a Bonwit's housedress, but a housedress nevertheless. She sat down on the very edge of the sofa.

"I'm supposed to be out marketing," she said rapidly. "I can't stay. Ellery, you've got to forget you saw me yesterday with Van Harrison." Her blue eyes were almost black this morning.

"Why?" asked Ellery.

"You know why. Dirk would—He mustn't know."

"Oh, that. He won't learn it from me, Martha."

She rose at once, relief written all over her. "I had to ask you. I couldn't leave it to chance. You understand that, don't you, Ellery?"

"Yes. But about the more important things I'm completely in the dark." He made no attempt to rise.

"Ellery, I really can't stay—"

"It won't take long, Martha. Merely long enough to answer one question: Just what do you think you're doing?" Her lips receded; a total withdrawal, like the retreat of a turtle. "It isn't really as presumptuous a question as it sounds. I'm not exactly a rubberneck bystander, Martha. You came to me once—it seems a long time ago—to help you with Dirk. I didn't expect you'd do the one thing that makes help impossible."

86

"I know." The words came out of her as from a long distance. "But ... there are some things you can't explain."

"Even to me, Martha? I've listened to a great many secrets in my time. I don't recall ever having violated a confidence. I like helping people; it gives me a bonus for being. And I especially like helping people I like. I liked you very much, Martha, because I thought you were sturdy and forthright and honest. I'd like to go back to liking you—and incidentally, to avert a tragedy."

"Just because I made a date to meet an actor in an out-of-the-way place?" He could barely make out the words. "You know why I did it, Ellery. Dirk—"

"Was it for the same reason that you met the same actor in that hotel room, and on The Bowery, and in Chinatown—and other places?"

He thought she was going to faint. She actually felt for the sofa. But then she drew herself up, her lips came together again, the dark of her blue eyes became darker; and Ellery sighed.

"Martha, I'm not sitting in judgment. I only want to help. All right, Dirk's driven you into the arms of another man. You're in love with Van Harrison, or you think you are. Maybe you went off the deep end on the rebound, after a particularly nasty set-to with Dirk. And now that you're in it ... Is it that you regret the affair already but don't know how to get out of it? Harrison acting tough and your hands tied because if you break if off he may blab it around town, even fling it in Dirk's teeth? Is that it, Martha? If it is, I'll handle Van Harrison, and I guarantee that Dirk won't ever hear of it."

"No! You stay away from him!"

"From whom, Martha?"

"From—from Van!"

"Then you are in love with him. At least tell me this, Martha: Why are you hanging on to Dirk? Are you afraid that if you asked him for a divorce—?"

"Let me alone!"

Ellery was still sitting there when the clatter of Martha's feet had died away.

He sat there for an hour, a slash of worry dividing his eyes.

Then he went to the phone and called the Lawrence apartment.

"Ellery?" It was Nikki who answered. "I … can't talk now. Dirk's up to his ears in this thing. It's really going beautifully–"

"Whenever you can, Nikki."

Nikki arrived within the hour.

"What's the matter?" She was scared.

"Sit down, Nik."

"But what is it?"

Ellery walked up and down as he told her of Martha's visit.

"Nikki," he said to her upturned face, "I've spent a lot of time this morning thinking that talk over. Up to now I've been inclined to treat this business as an annoyance. I won't make that mistake from here on in. It's a lot more serious than I thought."

"Why do you say that? *Why* more serious?"

"I don't know."

"You don't *know?*" Nikki was bewildered.

Ellery went to the window and stared down at 87th Street. "Doesn't sound much like me, does it? No logic in it. No facts. Just feelings. Ghastly experience for a practical man …"

"But how could it be *more* serious?"

Ellery turned back. "Oh, in lots of ways," he said lightly. "But let's get back on firmer ground. It's going to be a race against time. Sooner or later Dirk's bound to smell out just what's going on. He's nose-down right now. It's more than ever your job, Nikki, to fight a delaying action. He's hot on this book?"

"Yes."

"Keep those study fires burning. Drive him. Pamper him. Flatter him–tell him he's the greatest mystery writer since Poe and that he's producing a world classic that will outlive *The Murders in the Rue Morgue.* If he has another spell and beats Martha up again, shut your eyes and stop your ears. Above all, don't give him any reason to get rid of you. If you're out of the apartment, we're through. Of course, wherever you can, cover up for Martha. Do you understand?"

She nodded.

"Personally," said Ellery, "I don't give a damn about Dirk Lawrence. I'm tired of self-pitying neurotics. I'm no mental healer. Dirk's brought this on himself. If he insists on going to hell on a shingle, I'll respectfully tip my hat as he whizzes by.

"But Martha's a different story. I like her all over again. She's headed for trouble from Dirk, from Harrison, from God knows whom else or what. I want to help her more than ever and she's going to get help whether she wants it or not."

"Thank you," whispered Nikki.

"And there's only one way we can help her—by breaking up this dirty business with Harrison. Crack it wide open and manage to do it without letting it get back to Dirk."

"But how, Ellery? Even if you broke it up, how could you shut Harrison's mouth?"

"That little problem," said Ellery, "is what I propose to go to work on, effective immediately."

89

H·I·J·K·

That afternoon Ellery telephoned Leon Fields's office.

"Mr. Fields isn't here. Is there anything I can do for you, Mr. Queen?"

"Who is this speaking?"

"Mr. Fields's secretary."

"Miss Loughman?"

"That's right."

"Where can I get in touch with Leon, Miss Loughman? It's important."

"I really couldn't say. Is this a confidential matter?"

"Extremely."

"Well, I handle a great many of Mr. Fields's confidential matters, Mr. Queen—"

"I'm sure you do, Miss Loughman, but this isn't going to be one of them. Where is he, at 88th Street off Madison?"

There was a silence. Then the woman said, "Hold on a minute."

Ellery held on.

Three minutes later the columnist's jarring voice said, "Don't do that, Ellery. Your geography question had Harriet changing her panties. That's supposed to be top-secret stuff. What's on your mind?"

"Is it safe to talk?"

"On my phone? Listen, chum, I'm on automatic wiretap-testing service. They check every hour on the hour. Shoot."

"Well, have you thought about it?"

"Have I thought about what?"

"What you said you were going to think about. Just before our parting kiss that night."

"You mean Harrison?" An unpleasant flatness came into Fields's voice. "Yes, I've thought about it."

"And?"

"I don't know yet."

"You don't know what yet?"

"Whether I've thought about it enough. Look, Ellery, I'm in a hurry. I'm packing to fly out to Hollywood. Why don't you call me when I get back?"

"When will that be?"

"Two-three weeks."

"I can't wait that long, Leon!"

"My friend," said Leon Fields softly, "you've got to wait that long."

He hung up.

Ellery wasted no time thinking unkind thoughts of Leon Fields. Fields was a law unto himself, not subject to the pressures of ordinary men. If Fields said, "Wait," you waited. Usually, it turned out to be well worth waiting for.

Ellery saw no point in moving to the direct assault on Van Harrison until he had in hand the force and armament to impress his will, as the military said, upon the enemy. What he was hoping for from Fields was a weapon. The fact that it was a secret weapon made its acquisition doubly desirable.

Meanwhile, he could only keep up with the lovers between largely futile attacks on his work. His desk was piled high with unanswered correspondence, unread manuscripts submitted to *Ellery Queen's Mystery Magazine*, and the cryptic notes on his new novel which were so old that even he could no longer decipher them.

He followed Martha to Central Park West and 81st Street and saw her meet Harrison at the Hayden Planetarium. He felt rather bitter about their behavior on that occasion. They went inside to view the evening performance. In the dark they watched the artificial stars, and Ellery was not touched.

They left separately, and they went in different directions. Apparently Martha dared risk only the time for an astronomy lesson.

The following week, as if to preserve the mood of space and flight, they met at the Idlewild airport in Queens. The wind of a departing plane whipped Martha's skirts about prettily as her lover embraced her.

She was nervous, and pulled away and looked around as usual; and he, as usual jaunty, laughed and kissed her and away they went in his convertible—away to lower Connecticut, to a country road with a beautiful house at the end of it, overlooking a slough of the Sound, with evergreens sighing all around like envious neighbors. And the actor carried Martha Lawrence over his threshold as if she were his bride, and Ellery—watching from the protection of a typical Connecticut boulder—backed his car around and drove off with a sickness in him.

In the third week he telephoned Leon Fields's office again. Mr. Fields was still on the Coast, reported Miss Loughman. No, she had had no word of the exact day of his return, but if Mr. Queen would care to call again on Friday …

Mr. Queen would, and did, and on Friday Miss Loughman informed him that Fields had flown to Mexico City on a hot tip involving a well-known crusader for good government and a matter of a highly aromatic eighty-five thousand dollars, and no, she didn't know when he would be back. He had said something over the phone about possibly having to hop over to Havana for a few days.

And Ellery ground his teeth down another millimeter and tried to console himself with the fact that Dirk Lawrence was working at a furious pace, with not a loud whisper of his jealousy disturbing the ménage.

Martha, too, was busy these days. She had completed casting of the Greenspan play and rehearsals had begun in one of the empty theaters on West 45th Street.

Van Harrison was not in the cast. All the roles were female except one, that of a boy of ten.

She was a thinner and quieter Martha, with a whip in her voice. One Broadwayite, after watching her run a rehearsal, reported at Sardi's that "Martha's found herself as a director. Something's happened to her—thank God." The memory of her first two productions was still bilious green in Shubert Alley. It began to get about that Martha had a hit in the offing, and everyone hoped emotionally that she might make back some of the fortune she had sunk in *All Around the Mulberry Bush* and Alex Conn's stinker.

Still, Martha found time to slip away, in the fourth week of Leon Fields's absence, to Jones Beach, where Ellery watched her somberly from the promenade through field glasses. She lay under a red umbrella with Harrison. Her bathing suit revealed a streamlined Martha, with all of the comfortable upholstery of her early marital years stripped away. She was almost thin. Ellery was not sure he liked her that way. A thin cherub sang no paeans. There was something sad about her figure.

Harrison was in a handsome bronze beach robe, his throat swathed in a royal-blue scarf. This concession to vanity was a matter of simple prudence; he would hardly put himself on exhibition before her against a foreground of all these hard flat young male bodies. But when Martha dashed off to plunge into the sea, he removed the robe, dropped robe and scarf under the umbrella, and lumbered into the water. Ellery followed him remorselessly with the glasses. Harrison undressed was a sight. His skin with its sunlamp tan was flabby, he had a paunch, the hair on his chest was gray, and his legs showed clots of varicose veins. While Martha dived and swam like a porpoise, Harrison paddled about dog-fashion, his chin rigidly above water. He had, of course, to keep his toupee dry.

Ellery entered all the facts in his little book, adding *J* to his alphabet and wondering why he was keeping the record at all.

And in the fifth week, with Fields in Miami– "He has a lot of friends down there among the permanent residents," as Miss Loughman put it– Martha and her lover lunched at crowded Keen's English Chop House on West 36th Street as if their love were licit.

"I can't wait for Fields any longer," Ellery told Nikki. "They're getting more and more careless, and we can't expect this sweet obliviousness of Dirk's to last forever. I've got to tackle Harrison."

It was a Sunday morning, and Ellery called Harrison's Darien number with the gloomy confidence of a man entirely familiar with the weekend habits of actors. To his surprise, there was no answer. He tried again an hour later, thinking that Harrison might be sleeping off a Saturday night. But there was still no answer, and none an hour after that.

Then he remembered how the great Van Harrison was keeping his oar in, and he phoned Radio Registry, leaving his number.

His telephone rang twenty minutes later.

"Van Harrison speaking," said the rich, pear-shaped tones. "I have a message to call this number. Who is this, please?"

"This is Ellery Queen."

There was a silence.

"Oh, yes," said Harrison pleasantly. "We met outside a tomb. What can I do for you, Queen?"

"I want to see you."

"To see me? Whatever for?"

"Put your mind to it, Harrison. What are you doing today?"

"I haven't said I'd see you."

"Would you rather see Dirk Lawrence?"

"Not that," moaned the actor. "Spare me, buddy. Of course I'll see you. In hell, or anywhere you like."

"Are you free right now?"

"I am not, Mr. Queen. I was good enough today to come to the aid of a friend of mine—poor wight—eking out his miserable existence as a director of radio dramas. Some idiot got the bellyache and had to bow out of tonight's cast. Consequently I am in rehearsal, and I am calling from the studio during a ten-minute break. Now would you like to know what size bloomers I wear?"

"When do you get off the air?" asked Ellery.

"At seven-thirty."

"Which studio, Harrison? I'll meet you there."

"You'll do nothing of the sort. A young lady who thinks she's an actress, and has convinced several directors of same while on an Ostermoor, is likewise in the cast of this dramaturgical turd, and since she resides in Stamford, I have contracted at great personal inconvenience to drive her home after the alleged performance. I scarcely think our conversation—yours and mine—will be suitable for a young maiden's ears. I'll be home about nine o'clock, Queen—I take it you've sniffed out where I live." There was a contemptuous click.

Ellery was waiting outside the glittery Darien house when the red Cadillac convertible slid up the lane.

Harrison was alone.

He got out carefully and came up the stone steps bringing with him a fragrance of bourbon. He did not offer to shake hands. He began to fumble for a key.

"It's my Jap's day off or you wouldn't have had to park on the lawn. Waiting long?" It was almost ten o'clock.

"It doesn't matter."

His hat had a dent in the crown and there was a smear of lipstick under his right ear.

"I couldn't get away from the little bitch. Hottest thing since Hiroshima. I'm really put out with you, Queen. Come in." Harrison touched a switch.

The living room was typical of the more luxurious Darien waterfront houses, big and arty and full of gleams on the side facing the Sound. There was a large terrace beyond, and an immaculate lawn going down to the slough. The lawn was set with wrought-iron furniture wearing a W. & J. Sloane look. A stainless-steel barbecue on wheels was drawn up under a grove of dogwood trees, and a portable bar littered with glassware and empty bottles.

The room was really two rooms with the common wall left out—a sunken living room and a dining room beyond on a higher level. There were brown beams showing adz marks, a magnificent fieldstone fireplace, and a precious-looking staircase marching up one wall. The furniture was California modern, rugged-looking pieces selected for their masculine air. The doweled wideboard floors were polished to a shine and covered with brilliant Navajo rugs. Everything looked expensive.

The walls were cluttered with photographs, most of them of a younger and leaner Harrison in portrait or costume, the remainder being of theatrical people, uniformly autographed to Harrison.

"Forgive the disorder," said the actor, tossing his hat in the general direction of the dining-room table. "These are bachelor digs, and contrary to the popular conception of Jap servants, Tama is no bargain, as you can see. But he mixes a fabulous martini and he's a wonderful cook. A drab wanders in twice a week and waves a cloth vaguely here and there to supplement Tama's tireless lethargy. And now for a drink, if Gladiola, or Hyacinth, or whatever her foul name is, has seen fit to leave any in the bar. She was here this morning."

"No one answered your phone."

"She ignores the phone. I suspect she can't write." Harrison rummaged in the redwood bar set in one corner. "Damn Tama! I told him

95

to replenish the cellar before he left. A party last night cleaned me out." He held two bottles up to the light. "There's a suspicion of vermouth, and the whisky is dangerously near the vanishing point, but I think I can manage a few manhattans. I'll get some ice." He disappeared through a swinging door at the dining-room end of the long room.

Ellery waited patiently.

Harrison came back with a pitcher containing some ice cubes and a muddler, and two clean cocktail glasses. He set about mixing the manhattans, whistling bird calls.

"And there we are," he said cheerily, handing Ellery a glass. "Now. What's troubling your soul, Queen?"

Ellery put the glass down on an end table, untouched.

"What do you intend to do about Martha?"

Harrison laughed. He drank half his cocktail and said, "None of your unmentionable business. I think that covers all the possible corollary questions, too, old boy. But if you have any doubts, ask away."

"Do you realize what you're letting yourself in for?"

A telephone rang. Harrison said, "Excuse me," politely, and he took his drink over to the big trestle-table standing behind the sofa. He sat on the sofa arm and plucked the phone from its cradle. "Hello?" He took another sip.

The glass remained at his lips for a moment. Then he slowly set it down. "Well, I'll tell you, darling, I can't very well just now. I'm not alone."

Martha?

"Yes, the appointment I mentioned."

Martha.

"But my sweet—"

She was speaking very rapidly in tones that vibrated the membrane.

"Take it easy, darling," said Harrison soothingly. "There's nothing to worry about—"

Again.

"But I can't very well—"

And again.

"All right." Harrison's tone sharpened. "It'll take me about ten minutes. What's the number?" He scribbled something on a telephone pad as he listened, tore the top sheet away, stuffed it in his pocket. "Right." He replaced the phone and rose, smiling. "I take it you insist on making your point, Queen, whatever it is?"

"Yes, I insist."

"Then you'll have to indulge me. One of those things—you know our gracious country living. That was the wife of a friend of mine. They're up the road at some house party or other, and Keith's fighting drunk. For some reason I'm the only one who can handle him. I'll run him over to his place in Noroton, put him to bed, and be back here in thirty or forty minutes. That is, if you want to wait."

"I want to wait."

Harrison shrugged. He left quickly.

A moment later Ellery heard the Cadillac swivel about and swish up the road.

House party ... wife of a friend ... Ellery got up to wander about the room.

It was a clumsy lie. Harrison would hardly have asked for a house number on his own road. Besides, the houses on these shore roads had no numbers. That had been Martha. Harrison had phoned her during the day at the theater—she was working her cast overtime to prepare for a scheduled Bridgeport tryout in August—to tell her of the appointment for tonight. Martha had been frightened. So frightened she had risked a call while he was here.

Van, I've got to talk to you ...

"Well, I'll tell you, darling, I can't very well just now. I'm not alone."

He's there, isn't he? ...

"Yes, the appointment I mentioned."

He's going to pump you, Van. We'd better discuss first what you should say. Get to another phone ...

"But my sweet—"

Van, you've got to! I'm scared to death. I know you—you'll start to bait him. You'll treat it as if it were a big scene in a play ...

"Take it easy, darling. There's nothing to worry about—"

There's a lot to worry about! Van, he'll get suspicious if we keep this up. Get to a phone and call me back ...

"But I can't very well—"

Of course you can. Make up some story. A friend up the road in trouble or something. Call me back! ...

97

"All right. It'll take me about ten minutes. What's the number?"

That was how it must have gone, what Martha probably said. And the ten minutes was the time it would take Harrison to drive into the business district of Darien to a public phone booth.

So much for Keith, the fighting drunk.

Ellery looked around.

And as he looked around, it came to him in a leap what an incredible opportunity had been handed him by Martha's call.

He was alone in Harrison's house, and he had at least a half-hour.

There were three bedrooms upstairs. Two were guest rooms–beds made up, windows latched, closets empty.

The third was the master bedroom.

Harrison's room took Ellery back to old Hollywood. Here, spread royally, was the great Van Harrison in his heyday. The bed was an immense circular piece with satin sheets and a monogrammed spread that alone must have cost several hundred dollars. The rug was long-haired and black, sewn together from the hides of a great number of unclassifiable animals. The entire ceiling was mirrored. The walls, done in white leather, were covered with photographs of beautiful women, all–from the inscriptions–devoted slaves of the actor. Many were nude. Uninhibited sculptures occupied niches here and there. One recessed shelf was filled with pornographic books.

An oval picture window eight feet across overlooked the terrace and the slough, and before this window stood a striking kneehole desk of ebony. On the polished surface, looking rather forlorn in its magnificent surroundings, there was a portable typewriter.

Ellery went around the desk and sat down in the white leather chair behind it.

There was some typewriter paper on the desk, and he slipped a sheet into the carriage. He typed: *Mrs. Dirk Lawrence*, and Martha's address.

They came out red.

The ribbon was the black-and-red type. Ellery looked for the lever that controlled the ribbon-shift. All he found was a raw stub, and this he could not budge.

The black upper half of the ribbon was frayed and worn; the ink had been pounded out of it.

He made a face. There was no significance to Harrison's red typing after all. The color-shift lever had jammed and in trying to move it Harrison had snapped it off. He had simply neglected to have it repaired. Having worn away the ink of the black half of the ribbon, he had inverted the ribbon and used the red half …

No, there was no significance to the little scarlet letters produced by Harrison's typewriter, and yet it was not without a meaning. A "satire of circumstance," Thomas Hardy would have called it. Life was full of such curious tricks, and it took a poet to appreciate them.

Ellery was no poet. Neither, he fancied, was Dirk.

He took from his breast pocket the manila envelope of the Froehm Air-Conditioner Company in which Harrison had enclosed his first message to Martha; Ellery had brought it along with some vague notion that it might prove useful in his tilt with Harrison.

The address on the envelope and the words Ellery had just typed on Harrison's machine were identical in every distinguishable feature.

He tucked the envelope back in his pocket, together with the sample he had written.

And he began to go through the drawers of the desk.

In the flat middle drawer above his knees he found a revolver.

It was an old Harrington & Richardson, a .22 Special with a six-inch barrel, chambered for nine shots. The blued-finish arm was a discontinued model; it had not been manufactured, Ellery knew, for over a dozen years. But this piece had been well-preserved; it was oiled and clean.

Ellery broke it open. The chambers were all occupied by their deadly tenants, high-speed .22 Long Rifle cartridges.

He was not happy. It was a disagreeable discovery that Van Harrison also owned a shooting iron, although not exactly a surprise. Men who made love to other men's wives would understandably feel the need of a more emphatic protector than a wide eye or an earnest tongue. It was true that great differences existed between a .45 automatic, such as Dirk's weapon, and a .22 revolver, such as Harrison's, but these might be considered to disappear, for all practical purposes, within the confines of the average hotel bedroom.

Ellery replaced the weapon in the drawer as he had found it.

The two upper drawers of the three at the right side of the desk turned up nothing of importance. But in the rear compartment of the bottom drawer he found a sheaf of letters, without envelopes, held together by a thick rubber band.

The handwriting looked familiar. Ellery extracted the topmost letter and turned to the end.

It was signed, *Martha*.

He began to read it:

> Tuesday, 1 A.M.
>
> My dearest—I know it's a silly time to be writing a letter—and in the bathroom, too!—and I suppose in my position I shouldn't be writing at all. But darling, I guess I never learned how to be a lady except in unimportant things.
>
> Every woman wants to feel that she's important to a man for herself, not for what she can give him or do for him. You've made me feel that I'm important to you in that way. I think that's the main reason—and I say this knowing no woman ever should—that I can bring myself to tell you, over and over, how madly in love with you I am. I never thought it would happen to me this way. Or at all. Because I've been hurt so terribly many times

That was the end of the first page. Ellery turned the page and read some more; and then he stopped in the middle of a sentence and went through the other letters quickly. They were all the same—a day, an hour, a salutation of endearment, an outpouring of passion and hurt and loneliness. And all the time he was reading, Ellery saw between him and the closely written pages the dent in Harrison's hat and the lipstick mark under his ear. And suddenly he rebound the letters with the rubber band and replaced them at the back of the drawer and shut the drawer violently.

He got up, moved the chair back to where he had found it, and went to the other end of Harrison's bedroom. Two big doors stood side by side, and he opened them. They were closets. One contained nothing but men's clothes—an immense wardrobe of custom-tailored suits and coats, running the fashion gamut from country casuals and sportswear to tails and–Ellery gaped–a black cape lined with red silk. The other wardrobe was filled with women's clothes.

Ellery recognized at least two summer dresses of Martha's and a blue suede sports coat of a distinctive shade which he had seen Martha wear on several occasions. He remembered Nikki's remarking once, with the awe of the budgeted working girl, that Martha had bought the coat at Jay Thorpe. He looked at the label of the blue coat: it said Jay Thorpe.

On the shelf lay several handbags, one with a solid gold monogram: *MGL.*

He noticed a white garment on the floor of the closet, evidently tumbled from a hanger. He stooped. It was a nylon novelty slip with the name *Martha* embroidered above the hem.

Before he left the bedroom, on an impulse he did not stop to probe, Ellery searched Harrison's bureau and the drawers of his makeup table, a heroic affair in ebony and white leather, with a triple mirror. He found them–a set of toupees, and two corsets.

Harrison came in rubbing his hands. "It's turned brisk out tonight. I should have laid a fire."

"How is your friend's husband?" asked Ellery.

"Blotto. I just heaved him onto his bed and departed. Was I too long? – Here, you haven't touched your drink. I'll get some more ice."

"Not for me, thanks," said Ellery. "And, if you don't mind, I'd like to say what I have to say and get out of here."

"Fire when ready," said the actor. He squatted at the fireplace, crumpling paper and fishing for kindling in a leather scuttle.

"Those may be prophetic words, Harrison."

"What?" Harrison's head twisted, astonished.

"Dirk Lawrence has an Army .45 automatic, and he's recently taken to practicing with it. I might add that he has several medals for marksmanship in his bureau drawer."

The actor tossed a length of firewood on the kindling and put a match to the paper. The fire flared up. He rose and turned around.

He was grinning.

"You find that amusing?" said Ellery.

Harrison poured himself a refill from the warm contents of the pitcher. Then he stretched out comfortably in a great leather chair.

"You know, of course, Queen, that what I ought to do is take you by the scruff of the neck and toss you into Long Island Sound. Who do you think you are, Anthony Comstock? What business is it of yours whose wife I take for a hayride? Martha's over twenty-one, and I certainly am. We know just what we're doing. And I'll tell you a little secret, Queen—we like it."

"Is that the line Martha told you to take with me over the phone just now?"

Harrison blinked. Then he laughed and tossed his drink down.

"I doubt it. I doubt that Martha likes it, Harrison. The Lawrence-apartment part of it, anyway. You're typical of the successful tom-about-town—love 'em and leave them the labor pains. But you're asking for a pain of your own. How well do you know Dirk Lawrence?"

"I don't know him at all."

"Martha's certainly told you about him."

"His jealous streak? They're all that way, old fellow. I'd be myself if I were married. In fact, I was that way when I was married. All four times. That's why I'm not married any more. Let the other gent wear the horns." Harrison reached over and upended the pitcher over his glass. A few drops slid down, and he frowned.

"Harrison, you're not dealing with the average husband. Dirk's a moody customer. Hopped up one minute and in the dumps the next. Manic-depressive. And he's been through the war. He's killed men in cold blood. How hard would it be for a man like that to kill with his blood heated up?" Ellery rose. "You don't interest me at all, Harrison, except as a case history. I don't care a hoot whether you live or die. I do care about Martha and, incidentally, Dirk. You're playing with TNT. If Dirk gets wind of this filthy business, you won't have the time to think up a bad exit line. They'll have to put you together for the morticians like a jigsaw puzzle. Dirk's a mean man."

"You scare the hell out of me," said Harrison. He tossed off the dregs in his glass. "Look, my friend. I'm no more anxious to get a bullet through my loins than the next man. I am very, very careful about Mr. Harrison's health. Mrs. Lawrence and I will not be bosom companions forever. You know how these things are … By the way, don't waste your time repeating that to Martha. She won't believe you. Where was I? … Oh, yes. At the first sign of danger, Queen, I assure you I'll run like a hare. That may leave Martha holding a rather voluminous bag, but after all, those are the chances we girls take, aren't they? Meanwhile, it's fun. Can you find your way to the door?"

He caught Harrison at the side of the jaw with a right cross that knocked the actor's chair over backwards and landed him on the hearth of his fireplace.

But as Ellery drove away, he felt no righteous flush. Of even small victory. He had achieved exactly as much as a man can with his bare hands.

It was not enough.

He never should have come without a deadly weapon.

L·M·N·

Ellery did not bother to follow Martha to her rendezvous with Van Harrison at Lewisohn Stadium or at Macy's–two dates which came only two days apart. They could only prove an alphabetical variation of the same dreary theme.

Dirk made different music.

Dirk was growing difficult again, restless and morose. His progress stuttered, at times stopped altogether. He began once more to notice Martha's comings and goings, watching her with the telltale quirk of his dark mouth, his glances black and wary. Twice he followed her. The first time Nikki was caught unawares and trailed him frantically herself; but that time it turned out that Martha was merely going to a rehearsal, as she had said, and Dirk returned looking foolish. The second occasion found Nikki prepared with a prearranged standby signal to Ellery. She kept him informed by phone calls along the way, and he caught up within a half-hour to take up the chase. On this occasion, too, Martha's destination was pure; but the incident made both Ellery and Nikki jumpy, and after that they lived from hour to hour.

"Where the devil is Fields?" This was Ellery's cry during that time, and he became mentally hoarse repeating it.

Fields returned from Florida on the morning Nikki phoned Ellery that the *N* message had come.

"Which one is that?" asked Nikki. "I've forgotten."

"Madison Square Garden."

"But that's *M–*"

"New Madison Square Garden, a purism exclusive with the guidebooks. Haven't you looked at her copy?"

"I don't dare go near it."

"When's it for, tomorrow night?"

"No, tonight. It's the first time he's set the date for the night of the same day the letter arrived."

"Then he wants to see the heavyweight championship fight," said Ellery. "What's her alibi this time?"

"She hasn't made one up yet. I hope I can keep Dirk home! What if he should decide he'd like to see the fight, too?"

"At the least sign of trouble, Nikki, call."

The columnist phoned two minutes after Ellery hung up.

"Leon!"

"I just flew in from Miami. Do you still want something on Harrison?"

"Hasn't your girl told you how I've hogged your office line?"

"I like it in English."

"More than ever," said Ellery, "and twice as fast."

"Okay." Fields turned away from his phone; Ellery heard him say something, and a reply in a woman's voice. "Look, what are you doing tonight?"

"Whatever you are."

"I'm going to the Garden to catch the fight–that's what I flew up for. Do you have a ticket?"

"I was going to try to get one this morning."

"Forget it. I'm arranging for a couple together near the roof, where those little ringside ears can't reach. I'll send yours over this afternoon."

"Right."

"Be there by nine-thirty. We'll have to talk before the main go. I've got to be on the eleven-thirty plane back to Florida."

"I'll be there."

Ellery hung up, rubbing the back of his neck. It felt sore but free, the weight having been removed.

He was in his seat a half-hour early, armed with his field glasses.

It took him twenty-eight minutes to locate them. They were seated far above the ring, a little below and to one side of him. Martha was dressed like a mouse again, and she displayed a nervousness to match. Her surveys of the vicinity were quick and secretive; between glances she froze to her seat as if to invoke invisibility. Harrison was enjoying himself. The preliminary in the ring was a slam-bang affair of two heavily muscled middleweights giving their all, and the mayhem seemed to his taste—he jumped to his feet at each mix-up shouting and punching the atmosphere. Martha kept plucking surreptitiously at his coattail, and he kept tearing himself free.

When Leon Fields came up the aisle, Ellery slipped the binoculars into the case and eased the case to the floor between his feet.

"Let's get going on this," said the columnist, dropping into the empty seat. "I want to catch the big one from ringside. What do you know about Van Harrison?"

Ellery sat still. "Only what's generally known."

"Know how he lives?"

"I've been to his Darien place. It's shore property, only a few years old, extensive grounds perfectly kept, a Japanese manservant, luxurious furnishings, he runs a new Caddy convertible ... I'd say, according to his lights, he lives very well."

"What on?"

"Well," said Ellery slowly, "I know he made a fortune on Broadway and in Hollywood when he was riding high, before the days of the big income taxes. He hasn't had a play for years, of course, and the only work he's been doing is an occasional TV or radio job, but I assume that's because an actor prefers death to obscurity. He must be living on the income of his investments."

"He has no investments," said Leon Fields.

"Then what kind of income does he have?"

"He has no income."

"You mean he's living off his capital?"

"He has no capital." Fields's clownish mouth curved. "He had the last dime of his big dough taken away from him ten years ago when he settled his fourth divorce. Alimony, the races, and his natural inclination to be the world's biggest sucker for every deadbeat who knew how to butter him up left him flatter than that palooka down there's going to be in one minute. When he hit the bottle and left Avery Langston holding the bag in midseason—putting himself behind the blackball—he was already in hock for almost a hundred grand."

"But he can't be earning much—he hasn't even had a movie bit for years! What's he living on, Leon?"

"You got the wrong preposition, bub," said Fields, his eyes on the ring. "He's living off. Off women."

The package ... the package Martha had slipped him over the table in Chinatown ...

"He's pretty good at it, too," said the columnist. "In fact, in my book Van Harrison takes the blue ribbon in the Fancy Gig class against the field. And believe me, chum, the competition is something fierce. There are gigs with looks, gigs who can dance, gigs who are soft-soap artists, gigs with real European titles–poetry spielers, art lovers, bedroom athletes–there's a gig for every purpose and a top gig in every class. But Harrison's got something the rest of the boys can only dream about. When a gal's got Harrison, she's got the whole historic tradition of the stage in her arms, from the Greeks on down. What dame who's beginning to bulge around the ankles, or whose husband lieth down in greener pastures, is going to upstage Romeo? Not an imitation, but the real thing? He makes them all co-stars in a private production, with the heavens for scenery, every night a second-act curtain, and no lousy notices afterward. And all it costs them is money. What's money to Juliet?"

As Leon Fields talked, a note of passion crept into his voice and the cords of his neck became visible. He stared down at the distant ring as if to look elsewhere would cause him to lose something vital which he was trying desperately to contain. Ellery was very quiet.

"He's been supported like a king by one woman after another for years. He has real social security, Mr. Harrison has. You were right–he doesn't have to work. But you were wrong about why he does it. He does it for the same reason he keeps up his Equity and AFRA dues–to protect his professional standing. His women being able to see him once in a while in a public performance appreciate his private ones more. A champ has to have a fight now and then or he loses his fans ... They'll be in the ring any minute now. I better get down to cases."

Fields looked away from the ring then, and at Ellery. The slender little columnist's eyes had no humanity in them. They were the eyes of a department-store dummy.

"I'm listening," said Ellery softly.

But Fields seemed unable to get down to cases. He was being driven by a wind of irresistible force and unknown origin. "Don't make the mistake of underrating Harrison," he said, and suddenly Ellery knew that Fields was not speaking from hearsay. "He shoots for the moon. Money is his object, and he finds it where it is–way up there. You won't believe the women he's had. And he's never been in trouble, never been found out, there isn't another newspaperman in the world knows a damn thing about any of this."

"Incredible," murmured Ellery.

"He even makes them like it when he walks out, which is usually when the doughing gets tough or there's danger of fireworks from the mister. A dream-boat who passed through their lives. They always knew it was too good to be true, so what have they got to kick about when he slaps their fannies and says so-long? They've got their memories. I told you he's big-time. *Not one of those women has ever squawked."*

"Then how did you find out, Leon?"

"Do I ask you where you find your plots?" The columnist's thin lip curled. "But I will tell you how come I've never given him the treatment."

"I've been wondering about that."

"Yeah. Well, it's like this: If I'd ever printed the name–or even hinted at the identity–of so much as one of those women, he'd have named them all."

"How do you know?"

"He told me," said Fields simply. "That makes me a reuben, what? How come Leon Fields takes that kind of horse puff? In fact, why shouldn't Leon Fields print all those juicy names himself? Fair question, and it deserves a fair answer. The answer is this. I was, am, and always will be in love with one of those women, and I'll scrub Harrison's back in that ring down there before I'll let him ruin her life."

Fields's hand groped and disappeared inside his coat. "Queen, I'm hung up. I could spoil his racket tomorrow morning in one column and incidentally put half a dozen saps on his trail who'd break every bone in his body, starting with his famous profile. But he's got me stymied. I can't talk, I can't hint, I can't even breathe. I've even got a vested interest in protecting him. Not long ago I actually covered up for him so a pal of mine, another newspaper guy, would stop nosing around. All I can do is needle the slob when I see him, and I've even got to be careful about that. That night at Rose's ..." His lips compressed, and he was silent.

A roar filled the Garden as the challenger climbed through the ropes.

In a sort of reaction, the columnist's hand came out of his coat with violence, and Ellery saw in it a plain white unmarked envelope.

"This thing has burned a hole in my pocket for a long time. I've reached my limit. I can't take it any more.

"I don't know what you can do with this, Queen, but I'm going to tell you what you can't do with it. You can't let it out of your hands. You can't let anybody read it–anybody. You can't repeat its contents. You can't do a damn thing with it that might wind up in its being printed."

"That kind of ties me in knots, Leon."

"That's right," nodded Fields, "but not as tight as me. That's where there may be a glimmer. I don't say there is. The chances are there isn't." He still held on to the envelope. "There's just one possibility."

"What's that?"

"You can try something with this I never could, because you're not me and Harrison hasn't got his knee in your crotch. You can go to these women one by one and see if you can't get one of them to break down, to expose him for the cheap, woman-chiseling he-whore he is. Person-ally, I don't think you stand a chance. And, what's more, you've got to play this thousand-to-one shot so that I'm kept out of it. It isn't enough for Harrison to get his. He's got to get his and not know where he's getting it from. If the attack comes from one of the women, and he can only trace it back to you, if he can trace it at all, then it's okay.

"If you want this on those conditions, it's yours."

Ellery put his hand out. Fields looked at him. Then he dropped the envelope into Ellery's hand and rose.

"Don't even phone me," he said, and he turned to go.

"One question, Leon."

"Yeah?"

"Have you any idea who's playing Juliet these days?"

There was another, and louder, roar, and in the ring far below the champion made his appearance.

"Are you kidding?" said Leon Fields; and he skipped down the runway.

O·P·Q·R·

A new champion was crowned that night, but Ellery was not present at the coronation. He emerged from the Garden just as the gong inside whanged for round one and he got into a cab and went home.

He kept his hand on the envelope and the envelope in his pocket all the way.

He put on the lights and made sure the apartment door was locked and he sat down in the living room without bothering to take his hat off. He opened the envelope very carefully, and he took out what was in it.

It was a sheet of cheap yellow typewriter paper. There was nothing on the sheet but eight typewritten names. The names were all of women, and each name was followed by a date.

He read the list through three times. It was incredible. Of a piece with the incredibility of all the smart, cold-sighted, all-seeing newspapermen who knew nothing about any of this.

They were eight of the most prominent women in New York. Their likenesses were standard inclusions in the fifty-cent magazines. Their names regularly decorated the letterheads of charity fund drives. They were invariably photographed in their ermines and sables and diamond tiaras at the opening of the Metropolitan Opera season. The Horse Show could not go on without them. They owned estates in Newport and Palm Beach and the Basses-Pyrénées. The combined wealth of their husbands and their families could be reckoned not in millions but in hundreds of millions.

And to each of these women, Van Harrison had peddled romance in a private sale.

Ellery thought of what the publication of these eight names in the pertinent context of paid love would mean, and he winced. It would make the dirtiest splash in the history of New York society. Not that he held New York society in special esteem, but it had always seemed to Ellery that the great beauty of the American way was that, under it, even society people had rights. Children would be involved, and teenagers in finishing schools, and innocent relatives on their yachts and at their hundred per cent white Protestant American clubs. Not to mention husbands.

He wondered which of the eight was the woman who, by merely existing, had tied the hands of Leon Fields. Then he knew that for a silly speculation. The answer was: None. There had been nine Juliets in Van Harrison's personal stock company, and Fields had protected the ninth even from Ellery by the simple expedient of leaving her out. A gap in the dates was confirmation.

When Inspector Queen, still wild-eyed, came home from the theater where he had viewed the championship fight on the television pipeline, he found Ellery already in bed, reading manuscripts.

"What a fight," the Inspector said, bouncing and sparring. "How'd you like it, son? Talk about Dempsey-Tunney or the second Louis-Schmeling slaughter! Ever see anything like this brawl?"

"Who won?" asked Ellery, glancing up from the page. And he felt under his pillow for the dozenth time since he had got into bed, to make sure the yellow paper was still there.

It took him almost a week—while Martha met Harrison at the Oyster Bar in Grand Central for one of their shortest rendezvous—to arrange an interview with Mrs. P—. In the process Ellery discovered how difficult it is for anyone not a feature writer or an advertising representative bearing a cigaret testimonial contract to see a leader of society. He was unable to penetrate the defenses of the social secretary, a young woman with a voice like confectionery sugar and a will as durable as the Chinese Wall. If Mr. Queen wished to see Mrs. P—, might one inquire just what Mr. Queen wished to see Mrs. P— about? Mr. Queen was sorry, but his business with Mrs. P— could not be communicated to anyone else. No, it did not involve a charity, even though he quite appreciated how happy Mrs. P— would be to receive a solicitation through the customary channels. But this involved a confidential matter. Might one inquire the nature of this confidential matter? One might, but if one were answered, the matter would no longer be confidential. Of course. Obviously. Then the sensible solution was for Mr. Queen to write Mrs. P— a letter. If Mr. Queen wrote Mrs. P— a letter, would it be necessary to state the nature of the confidential matter? Oh, yes, that would be necessary. Did Mrs. P— open her own mail? Oh, no, all correspondence was opened by the social secretary. But if the letter were marked "Personal"? Most letters were marked "Personal." Then what was Mr. Queen's course? To disclose the nature of the confidential matter.

At this point Mr. Queen made an impolite sound.

"We seem to have arrived at an impasse," said the social secretary sweetly. "I'm *so* sorry. Goodbye."

In the next three days–during which his notebook dutifully recorded a meeting of the lovers at the information desk of Pennsylvania Station–Ellery tried variations on the direct approach. At a great toll in energy and ingenuity, he discovered Mrs. P—'s agenda for a certain afternoon. He followed her from appointment to appointment, looking for any slit of an opening. But members of the higher echelons of society apparently were never alone except when they went to the bathroom, and as the day wore on Ellery began to wonder if even that was true. In the end he was grabbed by a precinct detective, who had been dispatched at the call of Mrs. P—'s chauffeur. It took Ellery forty-five minutes in a dingy stationhouse, and a call to Police Headquarters, to convince the desk sergeant that he was not Lightfingered Louie, the Terror of Park Avenue.

Ellery solved the problem at a stroke–one of those inspirations which distinguish the truly great from the ordinary mortal. He spent the fourth day rummaging in secondhand bookshops in the Times Square district. Finding what he was looking for at the end of the afternoon, he scribbled his name and telephone number on it, enclosed it in an envelope, addressed the envelope to Mrs. P— at her Park Avenue address, and mailed it at the West 43rd Street post office. It was a tattered, foxed old theater program of William Shakespeare's *Romeo and Juliet*, starring Mr. Van Harrison.

The next morning Ellery remained sensibly at home, but within reach of the phone.

The call came at eleven o'clock, which Ellery assumed was a few minutes past Mrs. P—'s rising hour.

"Mr. Queen?" asked the sugary voice, glacéed o'er with mystification.

"Yes?" said Mr. Queen courteously.

"This is Mrs. P—'s secretary speaking. Mrs. P— will see you at four o'clock this afternoon."

Mrs. P— was far handsomer than her photographs which always attempted to make her look ten years younger than she was and always succeeded in making her look ten years older. In life she was a striking woman of middle age with vigorous flesh and a very youthful eye, which as Ellery was ushered into her triplex apartment began to snap like a new-laid fire.

She received him in her famous drawing room, which had been reproduced in four colors on a double spread in *Life*.

"I'm not to be disturbed," she said to the butler, and when the butler closed the door she locked it and tucked the key in her bosom. Then she turned, and she said, "Well?" Her voice was iced, and there was no apprehension in it, just a distant contempt.

"I take it," said Ellery, "that the playbill I sent you, Mrs. P—, had considerable meaning for you?"

She said again: "Well?"

"Believe me, I understand your position. You had to see me, but you don't know how much I know. Mrs. P—," said Ellery gently, "I know it all."

"How much?" asked Mrs. P—, and now the contempt in her voice was not distant at all.

"This interview is going to cost you a great deal, Mrs. P—."

And Mrs. P— said again: "How much?"

"It's going to cost you all the courage you possess."

Mrs. P— looked at him, long and hard. Some of the fire went out of her eyes then, and they became obscured behind a smoky bewilderment.

"Sit down, please. No, in this chair, facing me. What *is* your name?"

"Queen."

"I don't believe—" she began doubtfully.

"Ellery Queen."

"Have we ever met?"

"No, Mrs. P—. I'm a writer of detective stories."

"I'm sorry," she said. "I have no time to read. A writer of detective stories? I don't understand."

"I'm here in a quite different capacity. My father is connected with the New York police—"

"Police!" She stiffened.

"Don't be alarmed. I sometimes work on a criminal case. It may be in the course of the regular police investigation, or it may be in a private inquiry. I don't accept fees; I'm strictly an amateur. I work on two kinds of cases: those that interest me for their technical difficulty, or those that arouse my indignation. The case I'm currently engaged in investigating, Mrs. P—, is a peculiar combination of both. My indignation is at the boiling point, and the technical feature of the case consists in the fact that I'm trying, not to solve a crime, but to prevent one."

Her eyes did not leave his face all the while he spoke. But when he had finished they wavered, and she asked in a careful voice, "How does all this concern me?"

"You could help me rid society of a dangerous pest and perhaps save a life. Two lives."

And now her eyes steadied again. "And exactly how," she asked, "would I do that?"

"By charging Van Harrison with extortion and seeing that he pays the penalty for his crime." Ellery went on before she could reply. "I'm entirely aware of the thoughts that must be going through your mind. You see the spectacle of yourself hounded by reporters and cameramen, held up to public ridicule, disgraced in the eyes of your family, dropped by your friends, and—most important—the object of your husband's bitterness and anger. You see scandal and divorce. In other words, you see your life wrecked, and you probably think me insane to believe you would agree to collaborate in your own ruin.

"But Mrs. P—, none of that would be necessary. You must have heard of the famous Madame X case. I think it may be possible for your name never to appear. No one will ever know your identity as the complainant except possibly the presiding justice, whose discretion I'm sure you wouldn't question.

"No, before you say anything," Ellery went on, "I think you ought to know, at least in general terms, where my interest lies. It's a personal one. I have two friends, and they're married to each other. They're relatively young, bright, nice, and until recently at least very much in love. There's been only one complication in their married life until a short time ago. The husband suffers from a jealousy complex. He's been trying hard to overcome it. Of course, there have been difficult times because of it. But, given time and their attachment to each other, plus intelligence of a high order on both sides, they would have straightened out their lives.

"Unfortunately, just at the wrong time, along came this man Harrison. The woman in the case has independent means–she's wealthy. He seduced her. I have reason to believe, quite aside from what I know of his former relationship with … you, let us say, that he charmed her into this affair simply for the money he could get out of her.

"They have been meeting frequently and clandestinely for some time now. I'm convinced that the woman regrets her mistake and that she would like to terminate the relationship, but fear that Harrison might tell her husband about it in retaliation or, more characteristically, see that it got to his ears through someone else, is immobilizing her.

"She's in a really desperate spot, Mrs. P——. If her husband, with his jealousy phobia, should find out, there will almost certainly be a tragedy. At best it would result in the complete ruin of two lives well worth saving, at the worst in murder.

"Harrison is a criminal. He's far more of a thief than the man who burgles your safe, far more of a menace to society than the gangster who shoots to kill. He ought to be put where he can't prey on women and wreck lives like a drunken driver on a crowded street. You have it in your power to see this done. Your friendship with Van Harrison came to an end only a few months ago.

"There's very little time left to my friend, the wife. Her husband is beginning to sense what's going on. Once it takes full hold, he won't sleep until he finds out everything.

"If you prosecute Harrison now, it will take him out of circulation. He will hardly talk about one woman when he is trying to defend himself against the charge of having extorted money from another with whom he had the identical relationship.

"That's my case, Mrs. P——, presented," Ellery said wryly, "by a sort of *amicus curiae* in the interest of common decency. Will you do it?"

Mrs. P— had been listening quietly, with no expression on her face except attentiveness. When Ellery had finished, she smiled.

"What makes you think he extorted money from me?"

"I beg your pardon?" said Ellery.

"And why do you say," continued Mrs. P—, "that he seduced your friend's wife? I don't think you know much about women, Mr. Queen. If my case was a criterion, your friend's wife went into it with both eyes wide open. Very few women over the age of twenty-one in this year of grace are seduced. Van is giving her something she apparently hasn't got from her husband–the excitement of knowing that she's the only woman alive. He has that faculty, Mr. Queen. In a real sense, it can't even be called false. He's a great actor and, amusing as it must sound, he lives his roles. I consider myself a lucky woman to have known him.

"As for his wrecking lives, again I have only my case to go on. He didn't wreck my life, Mr. Queen, he enriched it. If this woman's life is wrecked, it will be her fault, not Van's. She knew her husband was emotionally unstable when she agreed to have the affair. If anything happens now, she'll have brought it on herself. It's Van I feel sorry for, not her.

"Van extorted nothing from me. The money I gave him was given freely, as a gift. If he were the criminal you make him out to be, he'd have tried to blackmail me afterward. He hasn't done so. Perhaps it's because he's too clever, or because he can always find another woman, I don't know. But the fact remains he's taken nothing from me that I wasn't willing to give. If I have any regret at all, it's that our affair didn't last longer. We stopped it by mutual consent because it was growing dangerous. If I thought it could be resumed with safety tomorrow–and Van were willing–I'd be the happiest woman in the world.

"I think, Mr. Queen, that answers your question?"

"Mrs. P—," said Ellery grimly, "you're a remarkable woman." And he rose and waited for her to unlock her drawing-room door.

Perhaps nothing in the Lawrence affair brought Ellery so low as the misfire of the weapon Leon Fields had pressed into his hand. It was a scorching blow. He felt so singed that he did not bother to go out on the night that Martha met Harrison at the elevator storehouse in the middle of the Queensboro Bridge and accompanied the actor from there to some unknown but guessable destination.

Ellery had selected Mrs. P— as his first possibility because, according to the dates on Fields's list, she had been Martha's immediate predecessor. From a legal point of view, the more recent the offense the better the case. Pursuing this line, Ellery went after the next nearest woman in point of time. She turned out a dead loss, as she was touring Europe with her husband on "a second honeymoon," according to his informant, and she was not expected back until the middle of October.

The third woman, famous for her political activities, led him a chase that covered two thousand miles and wasted six days of his time. When he finally caught up with her, she refused to see him. He had come armed with another of Harrison's playbills, and when he sent it to her hotel suite he expected an immediate reply. He got it. The playbill was returned to him by the same messenger, and on it she had typewritten–and left unsigned– "I don't know what this means and nothing I can conceive will overcome my ignorance." She was known as a shrewd judge of character and a very clever woman. Ellery flew back to New York.

He discovered from Nikki that during his absence the lovers had met at the 95th Street terminus of the Reservoir in Central Park; that afternoon Nikki had followed Martha herself, Dirk having gone off to his literary agent's office on some business involving a reprint publisher. Nikki had followed them out of the park and had lost them to a taxicab.

The fourth woman, Ellery learned, was dead.

By this time he was desperate. He moved in ruthlessly on the fifth woman, who was married to a French count. The countess received him at the point of a sinful-looking .30 Mauser and told him with consummate calmness that, unless he stopped all efforts to involve her, she was prepared to shoot him dead and claim that he had attacked her.

The sixth, seventh, and eighth women were milder in temperament and gave him receptions on a less violent level. But these were the earliest ones and by now they were quite clearly old women. His references to Van Harrison, his noblest indictments and pleas, only brought nostalgic mist to their eyes. One of them said that she would as soon prosecute "that divine boy" as consent to do a strip-tease on the steps of the Cathedral of St. John the Divine. Another wept bitterly for her lost youth and said she "could never face him, looking as I do now." The last showed Ellery an antique Florentine pin, worth perhaps twenty-five dollars. "No one knows—and you can't prove—that *he* gave me this," she said in a defiant tone. "So I feel free to tell you that my will instructs my husband to bury it with me."

Ellery threw up his hands, went home, and burned the yellow paper.

S·T·U·V·W·

Ellery was a reluctant passenger the night Martha and the actor met on the Staten Island ferry. He had had no intention of going, despite Nikki's warning of the time of the meeting–he had run across a Rosetta Stone which unlocked the secrets of the indecipherable notes on his next novel, and he was hard at work transcribing them into recognizable English. "I don't see the point of it, anyway, Nikki," he said over the phone. "I can't learn anything I don't know already. And there's nothing, nothing I can do about any of it."

He changed his mind the next evening, when Nikki phoned in a panic to tell him that Dirk had gone out almost on Martha's heels, with no explanation to Nikki except that he was "tired of working" and needed some "relaxation."

"He's after her, Ellery!"

"Take it easy, child. I'll get right down there."

Ellery was on the upper deck when they came aboard. The glances Martha kept darting over her shoulder were aimed at invisible enemies. Harrison seemed to be reassuring her; he kept stroking her arm, kneading it, laughing.

Ellery saw no sign of Dirk.

They came topside and sat down in the stern, and after Ellery made a tour of the boat he returned to the upper deck and settled himself in an uncomfortable shadow to watch. He was trapped for at least two hours, the time it would take the ferry to cross the Upper Bay and plow back; and he thought with some bitterness of Dirk, ensconced in an air-cooled pub somewhere and doubtless enjoying himself in his Dostoyevskian fashion.

It was a muggy night, and the crowded ferry trundled through the bay in the heat like an old woman sighing. What breeze there was came piped from a furnace. Passengers squirmed in their sticky clothes and, feeling like a fly caught in flypaper, Ellery squirmed with them.

Only the lovers seemed oblivious. Martha was doing most of the talking tonight, with Harrison bent over, forearms on his thighs, listening. But whether she was making plans aloud, or pleading, or professing her fears—whether Harrison was listening with gravity or a smile—Ellery could not tell. When Harrison spoke, Martha leaned back to rest her head against the cabin. But it would be only for a moment, and then they resumed their roles.

Ellery continued to squirm.

They did not leave the municipal ferry terminal in St. George. Harrison bought some cigarets, that was all. On the return trip they sat near the bow. Martha continued her monologue.

Ellery yawned.

The lights of lower Manhattan were beginning to glimmer when Martha suddenly held something out to the silent man at her side. Harrison was lighting a cigaret at that moment, and in the brief flare Ellery saw what the something was.

It was a flattish package, like the one she had slipped to the actor that night in the Chinese Rathskeller.

Harrison glanced sidewise and down without taking the match from his cigaret.

He smiled.

His hand reached for the package as the match went out.

Nikki was watching television with Inspector Queen when Ellery got home. The Inspector took one look at his face and snapped off the set.

"I've been waiting for you!" said Nikki. "What happened?"

"Nothing. Dirk didn't show. At least, I didn't spot him." Ellery stripped his jacket off and sank into a chair. "There's something I've neglected to do."

His father grunted and went out into the kitchen for the pitcher of lemonade.

"What?" asked Nikki.

"She slipped him another of those packages tonight. That makes two I've seen her give him since this began. I'm beginning to wonder how many I've missed. I'm pretty sure those packages contained money, and lots of it. I should have checked before this."

"Money," said Nikki, making a face. "You mean Martha's ... keeping him?"

"Hard words," said Ellery. "But I don't believe there's any question about their accuracy."

The Inspector came in and silently poured. Nikki clutched her glass and stared into it.

"For this, Dad, I'm going to need your help. Nikki, where does Martha bank?"

"The Hamilton National, Sutton branch."

"Do you suppose," Ellery asked his father, "you could get a confidential report for me from the Hamilton National?"

"Report on what?"

"All checks drawn by Martha Lawrence in the last two months or so. Nikki, does Martha have a substantial savings account in the same bank?"

"I think so. One of them, anyway."

"A report on any large cash withdrawals from the savings account in the same period, Dad."

"All right."

"And while you're about it, you may as well get a bank report on Harrison, especially of his savings account. He has a checking account in the Darien bank, probably for ordinary purposes—I spotted a couple of blank checkbook refills in his desk the night I was there—but I also saw some mail deposit envelopes of the Times Square branch of the United Savings Bank and the 48th Street branch of the Consumers Savings, and those are the accounts I'm interested in."

The Inspector had the information in three days. Martha had drawn no checks specifically to Van Harrison, but she had drawn numerous checks to Cash for large round sums, and her savings account showed withdrawals of other large sums. And Van Harrison's savings accounts showed deposits in identical amounts. The juxtaposition of dates corroborated the affinity of the two sets of accounts. Some of Martha's withdrawals had no counterparts in Harrison's deposits; these indicated the likelihood, as Inspector Queen pointed out, that Harrison had savings accounts in other banks.

"Adding them all up, Ellery, she's forked over around fifty grand to this Romeo in the last couple of months. Man, that's sex appeal."

"How can she be such a fool!" wailed Nikki. "Can't she see that's all he's after?"

"How long would you say, Nikki, she can keep this up?" asked the Inspector.

"Too long. Martha has a fortune. I suppose fifty thousand dollars doesn't seem like awfully much to her. But if Dirk ever finds out–!"

Ellery said nothing. He kept looking at the bank reports and worrying the knuckles of his thumbs.

A few days later Nikki came to him in distress.

"This morning, when I got the mail, Dirk almost caught me opening the *T* letter. He's begun to get up early, something he hasn't done since I came. And Martha's attitude toward me–it's become strained, resentful. I'd leave today if I didn't feel I oughtn't to until I'm forced out. But you …"

Ellery massaged the back of her neck. "No," he said, "it's more important than ever to stick it out."

"Ellery …"

"Yes, Nik."

"I think he knows … more than we thought he did."

Ellery's hand stopped. "What makes you say that?"

"He caught Martha looking into the guidebook this morning."

"The Maas? How? How did it happen?"

"We were in the study with the door to the living room shut. I was at the typewriter and he was walking around dictating. It wasn't going well–he didn't seem to have his mind on it. As if he were listening for something." Nikki moistened her lips. "All of a sudden he ran over to the door and yanked it open. Martha was at the bookshelf, turning the pages of the guidebook. I thought she would faint–I know I almost did. Dirk said in a funny voice, 'What are you doing, Marty?' She said, 'Nothing–nothing, dear. I was just looking up something.' 'In what? What's that book?' he said. She did the only thing I suppose she could do–she pretended to get angry and said, 'Does it matter?' And out she marched in a huff, with the book under her arm. I suppose by now she's copied

122

out the rest of the code places and destroyed the book. Only–it's too late, Ellery."

"He said something to you?"

"He didn't have to. He shut the door and when he turned around his mouth was twisted at the corner–you know the trick he has. It was a sort of knowing twist …" Nikki shivered. "I can't explain it, I only know what it meant. It meant he knew all about the book. It meant …"

"That he's probably taken a list of the ringed places." Ellery slowly reached for his pipe. "And if that's the case, I'd better start trailing *him.*"

The Trinity Church tryst, according to Harrison's latest note, was to be at nine o'clock the following night. Martha left early that morning for an all-day rehearsal, saying, "Don't wait dinner for me. I don't know what time I'll be back." Dirk said, "All right," in a quiet way, and he spent most of the day struggling with his novel. At six-thirty he said, "That's enough for today, Nikki. I think I'll go out for dinner," and he went into his bedroom and shut the door. Nikki waited until she heard the shower running, then she phoned Ellery. By the time Dirk left the apartment, Ellery was parked around the corner.

Dirk walked over to his garage. A few minutes later he rolled out at the wheel of his Buick Roadmaster, a gift from Martha.

He drove slowly south. Ellery had no difficulty following him.

At 14th Street Dirk swung west. When he got to Union Square he turned south again, into Broadway. He parked near East 7th Street and walked around the corner to McSorley's Old Ale House, one of the few spots in New York which barred women. It seemed to Ellery symbolic, and the symbolism ominous.

When Dirk came out he drove downtown at a faster pace, as if he were getting impatient. By this time it was growing dark.

It was twenty minutes to nine when the Buick turned into Pine Street and parked. Broadway was quiet and Trinity Place was deserted.

Dirk got out. He peered across the street for a moment, then he walked restlessly down to the corner of Wall Street, crossed Broadway, and walked back up the other side to the silent church. Ellery, watching from the southeast corner of Broadway and Cedar Street, saw him walk up to the door and disappear in the shadows.

The hands of Ellery's wristwatch crept toward the hour mark. Ellery felt tight all over. He had tried to find out if Dirk's .45 was gone from its drawer, but Nikki had had no time to check. If Dirk had taken it with him …

At two minutes to nine Ellery pulled his hat lower and crossed Broadway. He would have to chance Dirk's recognizing him.

As he reached the opposite sidewalk a car bore down from the direction of City Hall Park and slid to rest outside the churchyard near the corner of Wall Street. It was the red convertible. Harrison was alone.

Dirk stepped out of the shadows of the church and drifted, across Broadway toward Pine Street. Ellery let his breath out.

Ellery strode back up Broadway toward his own car. He had almost reached it when a taxi sped by. It was Martha.

Dirk saw her, too. He disappeared on the run, toward his Buick. But he was too late. The cab slammed to a stop, Martha jumped out, she tumbled into the convertible, and it roared away.

Harrison had kept his motor running.

By the time the Buick swung into Broadway, the convertible had turned into Exchange Place and was gone.

Dirk raced up and down and up the dark cross streets of the financial district as if he were demented.

"Just when he got on to this," Ellery said to Nikki the next time she was able to slip away, "I don't know. But he's on to it, and he's not making a scene because he doesn't want Martha knowing he knows. It's bad, Nikki, bad. What he's trying to do is …"

"Find out how far it's gone," mumbled Nikki.

"I'm afraid so. From Dirk's viewpoint, you can hardly blame him. He knows now that they've been meeting secretly, he knows Martha's lied to him consistently, and if he suspects the worst—well, who wouldn't? If I were in his shoes, I'd probably do just what he's doing. I'd want to know, as you put it, how far it's gone –. Nikki."

"Yes?" Nikki was all drawn up in the chair, as if she were cold.

"Did he have the gun with him?"

"Yes."

Ellery said slowly: "I'm going to have to come out in the open, Nikki. As far as I can see, it's all that's left."

Nikki opened the door of the Lawrence apartment and said, "Thank God. Another minute and he'd have gone."

"I watched her leave. Where is he?"

"In the bedroom."

Ellery walked into Dirk's bedroom without knocking. Dirk was standing at the bureau, his hand in an open drawer. He whirled. His dark face smoothed. With his back he shut the drawer.

"Well, look who's here," he said.

"Hello, Dirk. I hope I haven't dropped in at the wrong time. Were you going out?"

"As a matter of fact, I am. And I'm in something of a rush. Why don't you stop by tomorrow for a drink?" Dirk began putting his jacket on.

"Because tomorrow may be too late."

Dirk's arms remained aloft for a moment. Then they came down, and he said lightly, "What profound meaning underlies that remark, Professor?"

"I think you know."

Dirk looked at him. Then he snatched his hat from the bureau and strode toward the door. "Get out of my way."

"No."

Dirk's face was very close to his. "She's been meeting him on the sly. God knows for how long. Van Harrison, that ham has-been. This isn't a figment of a disturbed imagination, my friend. They've got a cute little code system worked out which tells her where and when to meet him. Right now she's on her way to the UN building–the rendezvous for tonight. The other night I almost caught them down at Trinity Church. They meet and they go somewhere. Where? That's what I want to know. What do they do when they get there? That's what I'm going to find out. And when I do … Ellery, get out of my way."

Ellery did not stir. "And when you do, Dirk, what?"

"Out of my way, I said."

"What, Dirk?"

Dirk said through his teeth: "One side!"

"I'm sorry. You're not going anywhere tonight."

Dirk's right shoulder came up. Ellery slipped inside the punch and pushed. Dirk fell over backward, landing on his shoulder blades on the bed. As Dirk bounced up, Ellery pushed him back again. Without slowing his stride he went to the bureau and opened the top drawer. He heard Dirk's rush coming and he turned around with the .45.

"Sit down, Dirk."

Dirk stood there, his dark eyes flaming. "Brother Queen!"

"All right, stand," Ellery said. "She's meeting this actor on and off, and maybe it's what it looks like. But I can't see the point of this gun, Dirk. What would it prove? That you're a better man than he is?"

"Yes!" said Dirk.

"Or does that seem like a sensible way of getting Martha back? It's no good, Dirk. It's no solution. For you or for Martha."

Dirk grinned. At least, it was a sort of grin. He drew his lips back, and the canines showed.

"Dirk, I'm going to take this gun away with me, and I want you to promise you won't buy another."

"You sanctimonious jerk," said Dirk. "Do you think you can sermonize me into turning the other cheek? Do you know what they did to me? Do you know what they're doing to me? Me! They're killing me, one piece at a time! And they're spitting on every last bloody piece! There's nothing left! Nothing!" He stopped, swallowing. Then he said, "You've got no right. Give me my gun."

Ellery said, "No."

"*Give it to me.*"

"No, Dirk."

The dark face twitched. Then Dirk looked down, and Ellery, puzzled, followed Dirk's glance to its destination.

He was looking at his hands.

When Ellery looked up, Dirk was smiling. "The hell with a gun," said Dirk.

He turned on his heel and walked out.

At three in the morning Inspector Queen was awakened by strange noises. He reached for his Police Positive and went into the living room on the run, his nightshirt flapping.

Ellery was sitting on the foyer floor.

"Greetings and salutations," said Ellery.

His father stared. "Hi."

126

"I'm sober," said Ellery.

"Oh?" said his father. "Yeah. Yeah, son." He went over and tugged.

"Gun," said Ellery, pointing a wavering finger at the Police Positive. "No, that's not it. I buried his gun in the East River. Heaved it. No more gun, Daddy."

"Come on, son, I'll get you to bed."

"Know what I am?" said Ellery. "I'm a pooped-out poop. Believe in heaving guns. So what? So no guns. So there you are." He waved his arms. "You *think*. But you know what you know in your heart? You're a pooped-out poop. Because you know something? He's right. Lot of people would say he's right. You know something?"

"Come on, son."

"Maybe I'd say it myself. Guns!"

Ellery put his arms around his father and wept.

There were no letters for the *V* and *W* meetings. Ellery witnessed them because he shadowed Martha day and night. Apparently the appointments were made from a public telephone booth, for which he breathed a prayer of thanks. It meant that for these, at least, Dirk would not be on the trail.

Martha must have called the letter-code system off.

"She knows," Nikki said. "She knows he knows."

Ellery saw her meet Harrison on the sidewalk before the offices of *Variety* on West 46th Street. He was not interested in them. He had eyes only for the terrain.

It was all right. Dirk was not there.

Ellery let them go.

Again, they met among the booths in the main shed of Washington Market, surrounded by the perfect vegetables and immaculate meats and jarred delicacies of the world. Harrison kissed her perfunctorily and seemed more disposed to stroll about, but Martha hurried him off, and they left by the West Street entrance to cross to the parking space below the elevated express highway, get into Harrison's car, and drive away.

Ellery had parked his car nearby, and he followed. He kept looking behind him. Dirk's shadow lurked everywhere.

Harrison drove slowly, avoiding the highway for the crowded streets. The convertible bore gradually uptown. Again it was Martha who seemed to be doing most of the talking. Occasionally Harrison turned to her, and Ellery caught a scowl on the perfect profile.

But when the actor let Martha out at Eighth Avenue and 41st Street, he watched her for a moment, and then he drove off smiling.

Martha went the rest of the way on foot to the theater where her company was rehearsing. She did not look back. She walked like a middle-aged woman.

Harrison's departing smile kept hectoring Ellery. It had seemed curiously contented.

When Nikki phoned that night, Ellery shouted at her.

Nikki did not shout back. She crept into bed and pulled the sheet over her eyes.

X·Y·

Nikki had seesawed through so many crises that, by the close of that first week in September, she was conscious of nothing more vital than a dizziness and a roaring in her ears. She could not have said what she was typing or even what day it was. Her life these days had the shimmer of a half-remembered dream.

Martha and Dirk floated in and out of a jumble of disconnected sequences. In all that week Nikki could recall no word or look between them. What went on in their bedroom at night she did not know, but in the waking hours their paths crisscrossed without touching, like the orbits of distant stars. Nikki was vaguely grateful. A collision would have sent her screaming into the night.

Remotely, she thought she knew what was happening. Dirk was ignoring Martha in order to control the direction of his life. He could not attend her and survive. And Martha ... About Martha, Nikki was in total darkness. Martha got up early and bathed and dressed and fled. She came home, usually after midnight, and crept into bed.

Dirk drove hard toward the climax of his book. Nikki heard him sometimes, long after she had gone to bed, pecking at the typewriter between clinks of a bottle on a glass. It was only toward the end of the week—just before the onset of nightmare—that Nikki realized he was no longer sleeping in the bedroom but was bedding down on the living-room sofa without taking his clothes off. When Martha left in the morning, he went into the bedroom and shut the door.

So matters stood until Friday, the fourth of September—Red Friday, as Nikki ever after remembered it.

On Thursday night, when Martha had got home, she tapped on Nikki's door.

"No, Mar, it's all right," said Nikki. "I wasn't asleep."

Martha had not crossed the threshold. "It's Saturday night, Nikki."

"What's Saturday night?"

"The opening. In Bridgeport."

"Oh! Yes." Nikki had forgotten all about the opening in Bridgeport. She had forgotten all about the Greenspan play.

"I'm leaving some tickets for you and Ellery and anyone else you'd like to have along. They'll be at the box office."

"Aren't you excited? Thanks, Mar!"

"Will you tell Dirk?"

"Tell him what?"

"About the opening. I'll leave a ticket for him, too."

"You mean Dirk doesn't know—?"

But Martha was gone.

Nikki gave Dirk the message Friday morning, after Martha left. His heavy brows came together painfully, and he said, "Opening?" Then he nodded and turned away.

Martha returned to the apartment just after four.

"Martha, something wrong?" It was so long since Nikki had seen Martha at home in mid-afternoon that she could only think of trouble.

"No," said Martha coolly. "We're having the final dress tonight, and I've got to change and get up to Bridgeport."

Martha disappeared in the bedroom and locked the door. Nikki waited until she heard the tub running, then she went back to the study.

"Who was that?" asked Dirk.

"Martha. She's holding the final rehearsal tonight."

"In Bridgeport?"

"Of course. The scenery's all up there and everything, I suppose, and they've got to become familiar with the stage—" Nikki knew just what was going through his mind. On the road to Bridgeport lay Darien.

Dirk turned away and after a moment he resumed dictating.

At a few minutes past five the telephone rang. The extension was at her elbow and Nikki picked it up and said absently: "Lawrence residence. Hello?"

"Let me speak to Mrs. Lawrence, please."

It was Van Harrison.

A sub-Arctic cold gripped Nikki's throat. She swallowed frantically. "She's ... she's gone for the day!" She hung up, keeping her hand on the phone. "Go on, Dirk."

"Who was that?"

"Somebody for Charlotte. Let's see, now ..." As she blindly scanned the lines of typing, she gave silent thanks to the fates that had decreed Friday as Charlotte's afternoon off. "I don't know, Dirk, this last paragraph doesn't seem right to me. How about looking it over while I go out and powder my nose and stuff?"

Before Dirk could say anything, Nikki went out of the study. She closed the door.

She had just reached the foyer when the telephone rang again. She sprang at it before the ring could be repeated.

"I told you–" she began in a fierce undertone.

"Hello?" said a voice.

It was Martha, on the bedroom extension.

"Martha." Harrison sounded peevish. "Who the devil was that just told me ...?"

Nikki heard Martha's gasp. Then Martha said in a voice so harsh Nikki was confused, "It's for me, Nikki. Hang up."

"Oh. Sorry, Mar." Nikki depressed the bar of the phone. The pulse in her throat was annoying her. Very slowly, she released the bar.

"–knew damn well you were home," Harrison was complaining. "I phoned you at the theater–"

"Van, are you crazy? Are you *crazy?*" The harshness was hoarseness now, an ugly sound. "I'm going to hang up–"

"Wait. I want you to come up to the house."

"I can't. I've got to be in Bridgeport. Van, for God's sake, hang up!"

"Not till you say you'll stop in at Darien." Harrison sounded tender, and amused, too. "Otherwise–"

"All *right!*" With a whimper, Martha slammed the phone down.

Nikki hung up. She was conscious of no thoughts, just a fear of great dimensions.

She went into the living room and paused to compose herself before opening the door to the study.

While she stood there she heard the clatter of Martha's high heels crossing the foyer, the quick door, the secretive little snick.

Martha was gone.

Nikki opened the door. "I hope I wasn't too long—"

Dirk still had the study extension to his ear.

Nikki thought she was going to die. His features held in the rigid expressionlessness of a bronze casting; for one blank moment Nikki thought he was dead.

But then he moved. He took the receiver from his ear and turned his head to look at it. The bronze shattered as he frowned. The phone dropped and dangled over the side of the desk, bumping against a drawer.

Dirk got up, pushing himself from the heels of his hands.

"Dirk. Dirk, wait."

Nikki heard the voice clearly. She almost turned to look behind her. But then she realized it had been her own.

He came around the desk, striking his thigh against the sharp corner but paying no attention.

"Dirk, where are you going?"

He came soberly across the study, with a sort of thoughtful purpose, as if to touch her, or say something important. When he was one step away, Nikki realized that he did not even know she was there.

"Dirk!" She seized his arm.

He simply walked through her and the doorway and the living room. Nikki hung on. The arm in her grip was swollen and quivering.

He went into the bedroom and over to the bureau and opened the top drawer. After a moment he looked puzzled and hurt.

"Oh, yes," he said. His face cleared. "He took it."

"I'll phone Ellery, Dirk," Nikki heard herself babbling. "You just wait here. Just one minute. When Ellery gets here—"

His arm moved and Nikki felt something flat and solid come up against her spine and the back of her head with a crash. Dirk wavered and became fluid and then the whole room went under water and after a while Nikki opened her eyes to find herself staring straight up at the plaster cupids around the ceiling fixture.

She scrambled to her feet, looking around wildly.

"Dirk!"

He was not in the bedroom.

"Dirk!"

Or the bathroom.

"Dirk!" Nikki scampered through the apartment, shrieking his name. But Dirk was gone, too.

The next thing Nikki knew she was railing at the telephone operator in a haughty voice for not hurrying the Darien call, and a woman's voice was saying in her ear far away, "But the line is busy. Shall I try the number again in a few minutes?"

"Oh, no, damn it," Nikki heard herself sob, and then, somehow, there was Ellery's voice, and she was sobbing. "No, Dirk's left, he's left, and I can't get a connection with Darien—the line is busy, busy—I wanted to warn Harrison, head off Martha—he's probably left the phone off the hook so he won't be disturbed, damn his soul to hell … he's getting ready to play the great lover, he's setting his cheap little stage …"

"Nikki," said Ellery, "wait, wait."

But Nikki sobbed: "If he knows about Harrison, he knows where Harrison lives. He's bound to have looked it up. He's after them, Ellery, he's gone after them. He acted so—so—"

"Nikki! Nikki, listen to me," said Ellery. "Are you listening?"

"Yes," Nikki sobbed.

"We'll have to take the West Side Highway as the shortest route—if I came east and south to pick you up we'd waste time. Get into a cab and come right over here. I'll be in front of the house in the car. Do you understand, Nikki? Come just as you are. This minute."

Ellery drove up the West Side Highway at a carefully calculated pace, fast and slow by turns, weaving the car in and out of traffic like a tailor plying his needle.

"Faster, Ellery!"

"No, we don't want to be picked up. A stop for a ticket might be fatal. Let Dirk take the chances. He's probably racing."

"Oh, I hope they stop him, I hope they throw the book at him … You're sure, Ellery? You're sure it was still busy?"

"I kept at it until I had to go downstairs. Harrison left the receiver off the hook, all right."

Traffic lightened after Ellery made the turnoff into the Cross County and Hutchinson River Parkways, but the Westchester police cars were numerous here and he could not step up his speed. Nikki, tearing her nails, kept wondering how he could be so calm. Mount Vernon, New Rochelle, Larchmont, Mamaroneck ... the signs moved by sluggishly, like a parade of old ladies.

"There he is!" Nikki screamed. A black Buick Roadmaster was drawn up on the grass; a New York State trooper was writing a ticket on the fender. But as Ellery braked past, Nikki saw that the man behind the wheel had an oystershell face and gray hair and fat fair hands with a diamond on one finger.

Then they were in Connecticut, on the Merritt Parkway.

It was interminable. Nikki closed her eyes ...

She came to with a start. They were off the Parkway, careening down a narrow twisting blacktop road at high speed.

"You slept."

"I couldn't have," Nikki moaned.

"We're almost there."

Dirk's Buick was up on Harrison's perfect lawn at a crazy angle, a foot from the stone steps.

The Buick was empty.

The front door of the house stood open.

Ellery sprang up the steps and into Harrison's living room. A small wiry man in a black suit and bow tie was rattling the telephone. His slant eyes bulged. "I call police," he said excitedly. "I call police!"

By the time Nikki scrambled in, Ellery was three quarters of the way up the stairs. He was shouting, "Dirk, stop, stop!" Furniture, glass were breaking overhead.

Ellery streaked down the hall to the master bedroom.

Martha lay at the foot of the circular bed. One skirmish in the battle had flung her there. Her dress was disordered; she kept plucking at it witlessly. Her eyes were animal with horror.

Dirk and Van Harrison were fighting up and down the bedroom with fists and knees and teeth. Harrison's toupee had been torn from his scalp; it hung crazily over one ear. One cheek was scraped and scratched. Dirk's nose was streaming; some of his blood was on Harrison.

Harrison was in a dressing gown. It was ripped; it kept tripping him up.

The room was a shambles. The mirrored ceiling was smashed in two places; glass was strewn all over the black fur rug. They had been hurling the nude sculptures at each other; the oval picture window beyond the ebony desk was shattered where a nymph had gone through, and fragments of broken statuary littered the room. A chair lay in pieces. Two lamps had been knocked over, and some of the photographs had fallen from the walls.

Ellery lowered his chin and charged.

For a moment the struggle was three-cornered. He had managed to get between them and they were both tearing at him, snarling like dogs. They punched and strained and lurched and clawed across the room to the desk and knocked the portable typewriter to the floor. A fist hit Ellery and he stumbled over the typewriter and staggered backwards, trying to keep his balance. His head slammed against the wall and he slid to the floor, dazed, beside the bed.

From this position, as helpless as Nikki frozen in the doorway on the other side of the bed, Ellery watched the climax of the nightmare.

The collision of the three thrashing bodies with the desk had shoved open the flat middle drawer.

When Ellery could focus, he saw Van Harrison on the rug before the desk, clutching his groin, his lips curled in agony. Dirk was prone on the desk, where he had been flung in the last savage exchange. His right arm was stretched out and lay in the open drawer. His mouth was open and the blood from his nose dripped over his bruised lips and chin and stained his teeth.

Ellery saw Dirk's head come around and fix on something in the drawer which his hand was touching. His hand came up and his body came up after it, and he looked down at the thing he was clutching.

It was Harrison's .22.

Harrison lurched to his feet, plunged. Dirk shot five times. Red holes appeared at Harrison's throat, chest, abdomen. Two of the bullets dissolved the mirror over the bureau.

Martha screamed.

Dirk turned in a glassy way toward the bed. The gun went off again, and again, and again, and again. After the ninth shot there were no more explosions, but he kept squeezing the trigger.

Ellery staggered to his feet.

"You fool. You fool."

Martha lay on Harrison's bed as if she had been flung there from a great height. A convulsion of arms and legs stilled as Ellery turned to her. Red stains were spreading swiftly over her head and dress. He bent over her. He could hear her breath.

There was a thud behind him, and he turned. The revolver had slipped from Dirk's hand. Dirk toppled to the floor and lay quiet.

"Nikki."

Nikki did not move.

"Nikki." Ellery stepped over Dirk's legs, skirted Harrison's body, went around the bed to the doorway and slapped Nikki's face, hard. She whimpered and put her hand to her cheek. "Go downstairs now. Get on the phone. Call the hospital–Stamford or Norwalk. Emergency. She's still alive. Then call the police if Tama hasn't got through." He talked in a loud, clear voice, as if she were hard of hearing.

He spun her around and pushed.

Nikki stumbled along the hall and groped her way down the stairs.

Ellery turned to face back into the room and almost fainted.

Van Harrison, who should have been dead, was on his hands and knees, inching his way toward the wall, dyeing the black rug as he moved. He reached the wall and clawed at it. Mewing sounds were coming from his torn throat. The effort brought on a hemorrhage, and he collapsed at the baseboard, his face pressed against the white leather.

"Stop!" Ellery sprang across the room. "Harrison, don't move again. *Don't move.* They'll be here for you soon–"

The actor raised his face a little, and Ellery saw his eyes. They were trying to express something his shattered throat could not–the certain imminence of death, perhaps, and something else Ellery could not define at all.

Harrison's fingers fluttered to his chest, his abdomen, as if to specify his wounds and mark them clear. Blood got all over his hand. He looked down at it, surprised. Then something new came into his eyes, a look–Ellery would have sworn–of pleasure.

Harrison rolled over to face the wall.

He hemorrhaged again.

"For God's sake, Harrison, lie still."

The actor raised his bloody hand with the other, steering it to the wall, holding it there. His forefinger was stiffly pointed.

The finger made a shaky, downward, diagonal red stroke on the white leather, from upper right to lower left:

$$/$$

He was trying to write something.

His hand dropped and fumbled at his stomach.

Red ink, thought Ellery. He's going for more red ink.

Ellery dropped to his knees, He braced Harrison at the armpits The replenished finger came slowly up and wrote again, another downward diagonal which began this time at the upper left and wobbled to the lower right, crossing the first mark en route:

$$X$$

Washington Market ... Washington ... W. The last meeting with Martha had been *W* in Harrison's code.

W ... X ...

Again. He was struggling again.

He wanted to write more.

Ellery helped him. He helped dip the rigid finger in fresh blood. He raised the heavy arm, held it steady.

Another downward stroke. Beside the *X*. A stroke exactly like the first:

$$X /$$

And still another:

$$X Y$$

As the last downward stroke reached the diagonal, Harrison's body heaved in a great backward surge, as if he had been caught in an outgoing wave.

He remained bridged in Ellery's arms, stiffly riding the wave, for a heart-beat or two, then his breath came out in a red spume and he went under.

All through that night, and through the timeless time that followed that night, Ellery was inhabited by a ghost. The ghost had a dripping finger, and the finger kept redly writing over and over the twenty-fourth and twenty-fifth letters of the alphabet. It covered every surface of the inner man with its cryptic symbols, until Ellery thought he must burst with its corruption.

And he failed to exercise it.

Afterwards, when he looked back, it seemed to him that many con-fusing things had happened on that night, in all of which he comported himself with gravity and dignity and no faintest grasp of the issues. He had the clear recollection that the Darien police came, and the state police, and the county people from Bridgeport; that Martha was taken to Norwalk Hospital under guard and put immediately on the operating table; that Dirk Lawrence was whisked away, his mouth fish-like, unable to utter an intelligible word; that the wrecked bedroom and the ruins of Harrison were photographed and measured and the body carted out under the eye of the County Coroner; that newspaper people from New York City and various Connecticut towns and cities gathered rapidly in swarms over the lawns, hammered at doors, popped flash bulbs, attracted great clouds of mosquitoes and millers and crunchy beetles; that he was interrogated over and over, and Nikki, and the Japanese houseman; that some time during the night his father materialized at his side and re-mained there, pale and wary; that at one point Leon Fields appeared and by some magic won a few minutes alone with him; that at dawn he and Nikki and Tama—and the Inspector—were seated in some office in Bridgeport talking to the State's Attorney, who wore a jacket over his undershirt and no socks ... All these things Ellery remembered, yet he could not have repeated the slightest significant detail of the night past the point when Van Harrison died in his arms. Everything was clouded over by a red fog composed of X's and Y's, like a sort of bloody alphabet soup vaporized and darkening the air.

XY ...

The scarlet letters.

138

He had a vague inverted view of himself standing before the leather wall like a professor at a fancy whiteboard, pointing to the bloody *XY* and explaining patiently Harrison's code, up to and including the brief meeting at Washington Market; but even that had no real existence, because he had been unable to tell them why Harrison had fought death back in order to paint those symbols on his wall.

There was another memory, of Nikki and the Inspector and himself standing inside the screening curtains surrounding a bed in the emergency room of the Norwalk Hospital, watching Martha breathe. There was very little of her to see, because of the bandages on her face and the tight hospital precision of the sheets, with other bandages beneath. It seemed to Ellery that Nikki had kept saying over and over, above the noisy engine behind the bandages, that Martha needed a specialist, a specialist, and that he had kept assuring Nikki the specialist was there, at the other side of the bed, and a number of other very competent medical men, too. And that somebody told them it was touch and go, but while there was life there was hope. And that now they really must go.

But that memory was all mixed up with Nikki's eyes turning over as her knees buckled. And then there was the long drive home … Nikki curled up in his own bed … the reporters … and, much later, the inquest …

The next day Nikki went back to Norwalk, where she took a room. Martha was still alive; the hospital people said this as if it were very good news. She could not be seen. Nikki camped in the corridor.

The only reality of that time was Van Harrison, who was dead. *XY* …

Yes, the next meeting place was to have been code *X*–a Mexican restaurant on West 46th Street. And after that, code *Y*–the great playing field of the New York Yankees.

But why should the next two meeting places have seized and held Harrison's dying attention? Was something to have taken place as a result of those meetings–something unprecedented which Harrison wanted Ellery to learn?

Ellery went down to West 46th Street and he stood outside the Xochitl Restaurant, with its green neon sign and its kneeling Indian figure and its front window surrounded by creamy green tile. And he shook his head, and went in, and made inquiries, and came away in the same red-toned darkness. Van Harrison was not known there. Martha Lawrence was not known there.

And Yankee Stadium? He went to Yankee Stadium, and he talked with club officials, and he went away still shaking his head. No one there knew anything about Van Harrison or Martha Lawrence beyond the outpourings of the newspapers.

XY ...

The papers were calling it "the Scarlet Letters Murder," with that affinity of the press for the elegantly mysterious. It was a rich case for the newspapers. A cameraman for one of the tabloids had put a ladder against the terrace wall and taken a flash shot through the shattered oval window at a dramatic moment. The ambulance men were just raising Martha onto the stretcher, and Harrison's riddled corpse was in focus to one side. The Scarlet Letters Murder ... They called it other names, too, not so literary.

And some of them, jumping the gun, pluralized "Murder."

XY ...

When the trial began, Ellery knew no more of the meaning of Harrison's dying message than he had known at the moment Harrison wrote it.

And for all the tons of newsprint which had been dedicated to the subject, not one word—and Ellery read all the words—suggested a single plausible line of speculation.

It was going to be a short trial. Everyone agreed on that—Darrell Irons, the famous trial lawyer who had been retained to defend Dirk Lawrence, the State's Attorney's office, Judge Levy, the newspapers, and—somewhat to their disappointment—the jury. There was no question about the nature of the crime; the only question was of the social advisability of the punishment. It was not a "lawyer's case," but a jury's.

Should a man be convicted of murder who has caught his wife and her lover in an adulterous relationship?

Darrell Irons's defense was the Unwritten Law.

"The Unwritten Law," Irons told the jury in his opening, "assumes that a measure of immunity shall be granted those guilty of certain criminal acts, especially of those acts arising out of the natural and even noble desire of a man to avenge his honor when it is besmirched by seduction or adultery.

"In this case you will in your humane wisdom be deliberating whether a young husband may not be forgiven for blindly lashing out, in a moment of agonized revelation, at the betrayer of his good name and at the conscienceless love-bandit who seduced her into a sordid bedroom romance and with whom she committed repeated acts of adultery. There is no greater affront to a husband's manhood than to find his wife in the arms of another man. You will not, I think, punish this husband for doing what any man or woman of you might have done in his place under similar circumstances. Let the husbands among you, ladies and gentlemen, imagine finding their wives in the bedroom of another man; let the wives imagine finding their husbands in the bedroom of another woman …

"As a law-abiding citizen as well as a member of the bar I hold with the State that human life may not be taken with impunity. But while laws are just, men are understanding and merciful; and in this case I say to you, ladies and gentlemen of the jury, look into yourselves, study the evidence as to the provocation, consider the damning circumstances, and you will surely find this betrayed and unhappy young man not guilty."

Irons then briefly stated the facts that the defense would prove, and he sat down with the indulgent air of an adult who has just been assigned an exercise in child's play.

The State opened its case by presenting the testimony of various law officers, putting into evidence official photographs of the victims and the scene, identification of the murder weapon, ballistics testimony linking the identified murder weapon with the bullets found in the victims' bodies, the Coroner's findings, the testimony of the Eye Witnesses—one Ellery Queen and one Nikki Porter, both of New York City—as to the actual events of the shooting … all the details necessary to prove what everyone in the courtroom granted in advance: That on the night of Friday, September the fourth, at or about seven-forty-five P.M., the defendant, Dirk Lawrence, thirty-three years old, by profession writer, of such-and-such a number Beekman Place in New York City, and husband of Martha Lawrence, had shot and killed one Van Harrison, actor, and seriously wounded said Martha Lawrence, his wife—so that her death also might ensue at any hour—in the master bedroom of said Harrison's home in the Town of Darien, County of Fairfield, State of Connecticut.

Irons's cross-examination was restricted to the testimony of Ellery and Nikki.

Part of Ellery's direct testimony had included the incident of Dirk's Army .45 automatic—a transparent attempt on the part of the State to lay the groundwork for premeditation. On cross-examination Irons went carefully to work on this point, eliciting from Ellery the ultimate fate of the .45, and stressing again the fact that the accused had followed the guilty wife to the fatal rendezvous carrying no weapon except his two bare hands.

Irons's case was in two parts. The first presented the jury with the clear and overwhelming facts of Martha's infidelity. This Irons did largely through Ellery and Nikki, who found themselves in the curious position of being witnesses for both sides. Into the record went the numerous details of Ellery's black notebook, naming dates and places of meeting he had witnessed between the wounded woman and her dead lover, beginning with the rendezvous in Room 632 of the A— Hotel; identification and reading of the bundle of love letters signed by Martha and discovered in the bottom drawer of Harrison's bedroom desk; identification of certain feminine garments found in one of the two closets of Harrison's bedroom as having been the property of Martha Lawrence—it was a long recital, and through it all Ellery carefully avoided looking at Dirk, who sat catatonically in his chair hour after hour, staring at the flag behind the judge's chair. Nikki testified to the code letters and the marked guidebook (which had never been found); she also identified the clothing found in Harrison's bedroom closet. And, under Irons's surgical questions, Nikki went over the preliminaries of the afternoon and evening of September fourth—the rash telephone call from Harrison, Martha's panic and hasty departure, Dirk's overhearing and reaction, the SOS call to Ellery, their futile chase to Connecticut.

Irons also called Tama Mayuko, who testified to at least five separate occasions on which he had admitted Martha Lawrence to Harrison's house and witnessed her retirement with the actor to his bedroom.

The second part of Darrell Irons's defense was devoted lovingly to Harrison. The lawyer called a parade of witnesses—in some cases the courtroom was cleared of spectators, in others testimony was given in chambers—who testified to Harrison's numerous amours with married women preceding his affair with Mrs. Lawrence. Irons put into evidence the figures of Harrison's meager earnings from his profession during recent years; he put into evidence Harrison's savings bank accounts and the contents of several safedeposit boxes, showing large accumulations of cash unaccounted for by his legitimate earnings and unreported in his income tax returns. And the lawyer connected Martha's withdrawals of cash with identical sums deposited in Harrison's numerous accounts …

At the close of Friday's session, Dirk's lawyer had still not finished painting the dead actor in his full gigolo colors. He promised more—much more—for Monday.

Dirk was taken back to his cell in the county jail on Bridgeport's North Avenue, and Ellery and Nikki drove to Norwalk Hospital. Martha's condition was unchanged; she was alive under heavy sedation, and that was all. They were allowed to peep into her room for five seconds. Her eyes were open, but she seemed not to recognize them. Her doctors had refused pointblank both Irons's and the State's Attorney's formal requests to take a statement from her.

Ellery persuaded Nikki to return with him to New York for the weekend.

Saturday began badly. The phone rang, the buzzer buzzed, all morning. Ellery, who had planned a quiet day for Nikki, spirited her away from West 87th Street and they went to Central Park.

They drifted for sweltering hours with no conversation. When Nikki's step lagged, Ellery found a place for her under a shade tree, and she dozed with her head in his lap. Occasionally she moaned.

XY …

He could not get it out of his mind.

Nothing had been made of it in court, by either side. It had been put into the record and dismissed as the irrelevant meandering of a dying brain.

But Ellery remembered the incredible effort, worthy of a meaning. It was relevant. Of this he was certain.

What could Harrison have meant to convey?

When Nikki woke up, they strolled across the park, and in late afternoon they found themselves among the beautiful little buildings of the park zoo. They found a table on the terrace overlooking the seal pool, and Ellery went into the cafeteria and came back with sandwiches and milk, and they sat there munching and sipping and watching the scampering children and the crowds about the tall monkey cages and the seals.

And finally Nikki said with a sigh, "I'm glad we came, Ellery. It's always so restful at the zoo."

"What?" said Ellery.

"The zoo," Nikki repeated. "I love that word, don't you? There's no other word like it in the English language. It's a fun-word, but to me a quiet fun-word. Even when I was growing up in Kansas City and Papa took me sometimes to the zoo in Swope Park, it didn't mean racing-around-fun so much as looking-with-your-mouth-open-fun, and dreaming about zebras and monkeys for days afterward ... What did you say?"

"Zoo," Ellery muttered again. *"Zoo."*

He was sitting straight.

Nikki looked at him, astonished. "Well, of course," she began. "That's what I just—"

"Zoo ... I'd forgotten about that!"

"Forgotten about what, Ellery?"

"Z. The last code-letter indicated in Harrison's book."

The look of pleasure left Nikki's face, and she turned away.

But Ellery went on, raptly. "Harrison wrote the letters *X* and *Y*. And then he died. Suppose, Nikki ... *suppose he hadn't finished?"*

And now Nikki frowned. "You mean he meant to add *Z*, but died before he could?"

"Why not?"

"Well, I guess that could be ..."

"It has to be! As *XY*, it makes no sense."

"*XYZ* ... I can't see that *XYZ* makes any more sense than *XY.*"

"It's an ending," said Ellery, waving his arms. *"The* ending. The ending of Harrison's code ... the ending of Harrison."

"What," sighed Nikki, "are you talking about?"

Ellery glanced at his watch. "It's too late to get up there today—"

"Get up *where* today, Ellery?"

"To the zoo."

"You're *in* the zoo!"

"Not Harrison's zoo," said Ellery. "Harrison's zoo in his code book was the zoo in Bronx Park. And that, Nikki, is just where I'm going first thing tomorrow morning."

"But what on earth do you expect to find there?"

Ellery looked blank. "I haven't any idea."

Some friends took Nikki away to Long Island for a day's boating, the Inspector had to be at Headquarters on a hot homicide, so on Sunday Ellery drove off alone. He was rather glad it had worked out that way.

It was a dreary day with heavy gray skies and an advance guard of thunderheads over the Palisades. It matched his mood, although he worried about Nikki. Portents seemed in the air.

He squirmed behind the wheel as he inched along the West Side Highway. His skin itched.

XYZ … It was possible. It was even likely.

But then what?

Ellery felt dogged. *Z* was the end. It completed the circle. So you hooked onto the merry-go-round and went along for the ride. Maybe there was a ring—?

He had never felt so foolish.

He left the express highway at Dyckman Street and drove north on Broadway to 207th Street. There was little traffic on the streets. He turned east on 207th and followed Fordham Road into Pelham Parkway and the Concourse Gate of the Bronx Zoo.

He left his car in the parking circle beyond the entrance and began his aimless odyssey. He felt a little more like Jurgen than Odysseus—searching for he knew not what. But Odysseus had adventured with swine; and because one objective was as good as another, Ellery set a leisurely course for the southwest corner of the park, where the wild swine rooted. He was that desperate.

On the way he paused at the Lion House to admire the big tankfuls of tropical fish in the Aquarium. He passed the Children's Zoo and the camels and elephants and rhinos. He almost went into the Question House at the solicitation of the sign. Would they know, he wondered, what Van Harrison had meant by his *X* and his *Y* and his probable *Z*? He decided they would not, and he went on.

The wild swine depressed him. Pigs with tusks. They gave him nothing.

He went on, bearing east.

And there were the kangeroos and the giraffes and the cavies, the bongos and the okapi, the great apes and the wild goats and the thrilling spread of the African Plains, where lions roamed apparently free.

And he wondered what he was doing there.

And so he turned north by west, and he visited with the panting polar bears and the biggest carnivores in the entire known universe, according to the description of the Alaska brown bears. And they gave him less than nothing, unless it was a feeling of relief at the steel bars that stood between him and them. And he viewed the moose and Père David's Deer and the Heads and Horns Museum, and the Monkey House and the sea lions and the Administration Building—and there he was, back at the parking space, having gone the great circle from nothing to nothing.

Ellery got into his car angrily and drove toward the main gate.

A line of cars waited to swing into Pelham Parkway. He crawled along, simmering as he stopped and started.

A park workman was busy at the gate, and because there was nothing else to do Ellery watched him. The workman was wielding a paint-brush on the faded lettering of the entranceway sign. NEW YORK ZOO-LOGICAL-something, it said. The painter was working over the first *L*.

Ellery sat up. But then he slumped again.

He wondered what was holding up the line, and he stuck his head out. Two cars had locked bumpers.

He settled back for another wait, and his glance returned to the sign painter.

L. O …

The painter started on the *G*.

And there came a stroke, as of lightning, and the heavens proclaimed alarums and excursions, and the rains came …

The painter shook his head, gathered his buckets and his brushes, and went away.

Ellery became aware of a great honking and beeping behind him. He looked up, blankly. There was nothing before him. He drove into Pelham Parkway.

Lightning again. And sweet thunder.

He drove in a daze, circling until he approached the entrance again, and driving slowly past the unfinished sign to gaze with wonder at the running paint. And he drove back to the parking circle, and he got out, and he walked reverently in the pelting rain back to the entrance–back to stare up at the sign and admire how the heavens opened and emptied.

A sign, a sign.

Ellery came to at a tap on his arm.

"You the owner of that car in the parking circle?" It was a park attendant. "It's past closing."

Ellery looked at his watch. It was almost seven o'clock. He had been standing at the entrance in the rain for almost two hours.

"We've been laying bets on you, Mister," said the attendant, matching strides with him. "Anybody stands in the rain like he was under a shower on a hot day is either waiting for a date or he's doping the horses for tomorrow's races. Or is something wrong?"

"Yes."

"Something wrong?"

"Well, yes and no. It's wrong and it's right."

The attendant shook his head. He said disconsolately, "Then I guess all bets are off," and he stared after Ellery until Ellery got into his car and drove out of the park.

It was wrong and it was right.

Exactly.

Ellery drove by habit, unconscious of direction or destination. And as he drove he went over the ground for the tenth time, from the beginning.

Yes, it was right. It was wrong, too, but now the important thing was the rightness.

All I need now, he was thinking, is evidence. Evidence that will stand up in court. Evidence to satisfy the State's Attorney and the judge and the jury.

If it exists.

If it can be found.

If it can be found in time.

He began to feel depressed again.

The fact that he now knew what Van Harrison had meant by his bloody printing no longer seemed important.

The important thing was: Could he prove it?

Z ...

At a few minutes before ten on Monday morning, Ellery stood at bay in Judge Levy's chambers off the courtroom. Before him sat the judge, the prosecutor, and Dirk's attorney.

"I'm given to understand, Mr. Queen," said Judge Levy, "that you have something of importance to impart before court convenes this morning."

"What is it?" asked Darrell Irons coldly. He did not care for the introduction of something of importance at a time when he was expecting a quick wrap-up and a quicker favorable verdict.

The State merely looked receptive.

Ellery chose his words. "There is the possibility of new evidence in the case, Your Honor. If this new evidence can be found, it will have a significant bearing on the trial. Would it be possible for you to declare a recess of ... say ..."–he tried to read the judge's expression, failed, and decided in favor of conservatism– "twenty-four hours?"

"New evidence?" frowned Irons. "Of what, Queen?"

"Yes, Mr. Queen," asked the judge, "what is the nature of this evidence?"

"I'd prefer not to say."

"My dear sir," exclaimed Judge Levy, "you can't expect me to recess a murder trial on your mere say-so."

"I have no choice," said Ellery quickly. "It's the sort of thing no legal mind would swallow for a moment without the evidence to wash it down. I'm not even sure evidence sufficient to bring into court exists. I can only plead my qualifications and experience in these matters. I give you my word, Judge Levy, there is no trick involved, I have no ax to grind, I'm acting for no one, and I'm aiming toward nothing but simple justice. All I ask is one day."

Irons shook his head, smiling, as if in all his years at the bar he had never heard such a childish request.

"Of course," began the State, "Mr. Queen does have unique standing, Sam—"

The judge rose. "No, I'm sorry. I can't delay the trial on any such basis. If you're ready, gentlemen?"

Ellery touched the prosecutor's sleeve and he lingered a moment.

"What the devil do you have, Queen?" he asked in a low voice.

Ellery shrugged. "Right now, nothing but a web spun in thin air. What are the chances of the trial's going to the jury today?"

"Not very good, I should say. It depends principally on Irons at this point. He seems determined to convict Van Harrison of multiple adultery."

Ellery looked relieved. "Then would you cooperate to this extent? I'd appreciate your doing two things for me: Have one of the exhibits in the case submitted to a lab for analysis, and lend me for a few hours' study all the records of Harrison's various bank accounts."

"I suppose it could be done with the Court's permission and under the proper supervision," said the State doubtfully. "Which exhibit?"

Ellery told him.

The prosecutor looked puzzled. "Why that one?"

"I'd rather not say now. If what I suspect is demonstrably true, you'll hear plenty before the day is out."

"I'm being paged. I may not be able to get to Judge Levy on this before the noon recess … Coming!" He dashed into the courtroom.

But he spoke to the jurist immediately. Judge Levy conferred with Irons, who threw up his hands and glanced heavenward. Ellery hurried out after the exhibit.

An officer took him to an empty courtroom. Ellery spread out the records of Harrison's bank accounts on the bench and set to work. The exhibit he had asked for was already on its way to the laboratory.

Forty-five minutes later he looked up. "Officer, do you know Miss Porter by sight—Nikki Porter, one of the witnesses in this case?"

"Redheaded babe? Yes, *sir,*" said the officer enthusiastically. Ellery scribbled on a scratch pad, tore off the sheet. "Would you take this note to her and ask her to write the answer below? She's in the courtroom."

"I'm not supposed to leave these things—"

"I'll guard them with my life. I have a far greater interest in them just now than the State of Connecticut. Hurry, officer, will you?"

When the policeman returned, Ellery read Nikki's scribble, and he nodded with satisfaction. "I'll be right back, officer."

He found a phone booth and put in a call to his father at New York Police Headquarters.

"Oh, Ellery. Is it all over?" asked the Inspector.

"Not yet. Look, Dad, can you arrange for permission to examine a certain account at the Equity Savings Bank, Fifth Avenue branch?"

"What's up, son?"

"I haven't time to explain. Can you do it yourself? I can leave here and meet you in two hours, with luck."

"Get on your wagon."

Ellery sped back to the empty room. "I've got to drive down to New York, officer. You can take these back to the courtroom."

When Ellery returned to the county courthouse, it was late afternoon. He dashed to a phone booth and called the laboratory to which the other exhibit had been sent.

"There's no question about that?"

"No, Mr. Queen. A minimum of four years, most likely five."

"Thank you!"

Ellery hurried up to the courtroom, glancing confidently at his watch.

The corridor was thronged. People milled, talking noisily.

"Ellery?"

"Nikki! What's all this? Session over for the day?"

"Don't you know? Haven't you been here?"

"Obviously not," said Ellery, a frost settling over his bones. "What's happened?"

"The case just went to the jury."

"No!"

"For some reason," said Nikki, eying him curiously, "Mr. Irons rested for the defense shortly before noon. After the noon recess, they had a short recross-examination and went right into the summations. The jury went out about fifteen minutes ago. Where you going?"

"To see Judge Levy!"

Ellery faced the judge, the prosecutor, and a poker-faced defense counsel in the judge's chambers. Nikki sat in a corner, searching Ellery's face.

"I'm not going to waste time in recriminations, Mr. Irons," Ellery began rapidly. "You pulled a fast one in the interests of your client. But from what I know about you, you're concerned with justice as well as doing a smart legal job.

"About the feeling of the State's Attorney's office and you, Judge Levy, I have no doubts.

"So we all want to see justice done. The only question is: Is there time? For all I know, with the jury already out, it may be too late. No—please. We haven't time to go into the legal technicalities.

"Listen to me. Very carefully."

Ellery leaned over the judge's desk. "I've spent the day trying to find proof of a theory that came to me late yesterday. As I said this morning, it's a theory I couldn't expect anyone of legal training to accept without the corroboration of evidence. I've found that evidence. It puts an entirely new construction on this case.

"The theory hinges on a proper interpretation of Van Harrison's dying message to me, which everyone has ignored so far because it seemed meaningless.

"The truth is, it had the most pertinent meaning.

"I myself have held three different views about what Harrison wrote on that wall in his own blood.

"The first was that the letters *XY* constituted the complete message he intended to convey to me. This one I finally discarded, for the simple reason that no explanation offered itself. As *XY*, the message bore no significant relevance to the situation, its background, or its climax.

"My second view necessarily jumped off from the failure of the first. If *XY* meant nothing, then perhaps the message wasn't complete. Harrison died just as he finished the short left-hand crosspiece of the *Y. Suppose he had intended to go on?"*

152

The three men looked startled.

"If that was so, what could he have meant to add? He'd written an X, and he'd written a Y. It seemed to me that the only logical extension of X and Y was Z. Was this message to have been XYZ? But just as X and Y individually led nowhere, so with Z. And they meant nothing in combination, as XYZ. I was stumped again."

"Wait, wait," said Judge Levy. "I've never been very quick at puzzles. Do you mean that if Harrison had finished his message, the element he meant to add would not have been Z, but something else?"

"That's right, Your Honor. The failure of Z forced me to an entirely different speculation."

"And you know, Mr. Queen, what Harrison intended to add?"

"Yes, Your Honor."

"Just a moment," said the State.

He jumped up and went to the door. He came back hurriedly.

"Nothing from the jury room yet. Go on, Queen!"

Darrell Irons shifted in his chair.

"May I borrow a soft pencil and a sheet of paper, Judge?" asked Ellery.

The judge produced them. Ellery bent over the desk.

"I'll repeat the demonstration I gave on the stand. This is exactly the way Harrison scrawled his message. First he drew a diagonal, from upper right to lower left, like this."

Ellery drew a line:

$$/$$

"Then, starting at upper left, he drew a crossing diagonal, like this.

$$X$$

"His third stroke duplicated his first stroke, but a little beyond the X he had already drawn.

153

X /

"And finally, beginning again at upper left, as in the second stroke of the first *X*, Harrison drew a short diagonal which just touched the long diagonal, like this.

X Y

"At this point, he died," said Ellery. "Now, gentlemen, there is more than one way in which Harrison could have left his message unfinished. I learned that at the Bronx Zoo yesterday. I saw a park workman start painting a letter of the alphabet on a sign. The letter was the *G* of ZO-OLOGICAL. But it started to rain while he was doing it, and so he stopped, leaving the *G* uncompleted. And it didn't look like a *G* at all; it looked like a *C*, because he never got to add the crossbar … Suppose," said Ellery, *"suppose it was the last stroke–the short one–which Harrison didn't live long enough to finish?"*

With a frown, Judge Levy began: "You mean–"

"I mean, Your Honor: Suppose Harrison meant to carry that last stroke *all the way down?* As, in fact, he had done in the case of the second stroke of the first *X,* Then the letter following the *X* would not have been *Y,* but …"

And Ellery completed the stroke.

X X

"*X,*" exclaimed the State. "Another one. Not *XY,* but *XX.* "

Irons kept staring at the paper. As he stared, his great gray brows drew slowly together.

"*XX,*" repeated the judge. "I can't see, Mr. Queen, that you've advanced an iota. It's the new evidence you claim to have turned up that I'm interested in. Would you get on to that?"

Ellery came back from the door. The jury was still out.

"Yes, sir," he said. "I'm getting to it step by step because there's a road to the truth and the evidence lies at the end of it. Let me put it this way: What else is an *X*, Your Honor, besides being a letter of the alphabet?"

"A Roman numeral. Signifying ten."

"Then *XX*—*two X's*—in this interpretation would signify twenty. Does the number twenty suggest a connection with any phase of this case?"

"Not to me," said His Honor. He changed his position in his leather swivel chair, glancing impatiently at the clock.

"Twenty?" The State shook his head.

Defense counsel leaned back and lit a cigar. He devoted himself with concentration to the removal of the band and the clipping of the tip.

"Then if as a Roman numeral the two *X*'s get us nowhere," continued Ellery, "we must look for still another interpretation. What else is an *X?*"

"Mathematical sign," snapped the judge. "Multiplication symbol."

"Then *XX* would be two multiplication signs? Obviously that means nothing. Is there still another meaning for the symbol *X?*"

"A cross," cried the State. "Two *X's*, two crosses—"

"In other words, gentlemen," nodded Ellery, leaning forward across the desk, "Van Harrison, physically unable to talk; realizing he had no time to write out a message, reduced what he wanted me to know to its most economical form. He began to shape the common sign of the double-cross. Harrison was trying to tell me, with his expiring strength, that he had been double-crossed."

The silence lasted for some time.

Then Darrell Irons crossed his fine legs and blew a cloud of smoke. "Double-crossed, Queen? How can that possibly have a bearing on the case?"

"I think you've known the answer to that, Mr. Irons," said Ellery, "for some minutes now. Harrison had just fallen with three bullets in him, mortally wounded. I had witnessed the shooting, and he knew it. Knowing it, he tried to tell me that he had been double-crossed. What could he have meant but that the shooting I had just witnessed was not what it seemed? *That, in being shot, he had been double-crossed?*"

"I don't understand," said Judge Levy fretfully. "I really don't."

"I think Mr. Irons does," said Ellery. "For why should Harrison have characterized his killing as a double-cross? A double-cross means a broken agreement. Logically, then, *Harrison had had specific assurances that no such thing would ever happen.* He had been promised that he ran no danger of reprisal, and that promise had been broken. Who could have made such a promise and broken it? Only one person—the man who had fired the shots, the presumably deceived husband. *In other words, Van Harrison and Dirk Lawrence had been working together.* The whole case is not what it has seemed to be—that of the unfaithful wife and the deceived husband. With the husband and the lover confederates, with the husband aiding and abetting the affair—*it was the wife who was deceived. Martha Lawrence, gentlemen, was framed—framed by her own husband.*"

Nikki got up. She looked ill.

"You'll have to excuse me," she said in a faint voice.

The men rose mechanically. When the door closed, they sat down the same way.

"Proof," said Judge Levy. "Proof!"

"I'll get to it," Ellery promised. "Just let me work my way down the road without interruption—is that jury still out?"

"Yes, yes. Go on!"

"Once you accept the premise that the husband was behind the affair, that the wife was framed by him, with the lover his accomplice, every aspect of the case changes. If it is, no longer a genuine love affair, then Martha Lawrence did not give money to Van Harrison as other women had given it to him, out of sexual gratitude, as free gifts. She must have given him the money because she was forced to. When a woman is forced to give money to a man, whatever the man's lever may be, you can be sure the word 'blackmail' is stamped on it. Harrison blackmailed Martha Lawrence into giving him frequent and very large sums.

"But Harrison was the tool of Dirk Lawrence. Was it Lawrence's motive, then, to use Harrison as an instrument of blackmail? Yes, but only incidentally. Because what did Dirk Lawrence eventually do? He killed Van Harrison and *he tried to kill Martha Lawrence.* If Martha should die, *Lawrence as her husband comes into her considerable fortune.* That's why I characterize the blackmail part of the plot, which Lawrence assigned to Harrison, as only incidental to Lawrence's greater plan–a plan that Harrison, of course, knew nothing about.

"It was big money Lawrence was after, and he worked out a ruthless scheme to get it. Whatever his early feelings for Martha were, he must have tired of her and come to detest his marriage. On top of this, he failed miserably to make a financial success of his writing career. So there he was, tied to a woman he didn't want but who had the money he did want. Freedom and security were Lawrence's objectives–how could he get both? And then he saw the way."

Irons examined the tip of his cigar; it had gone out. "By attempting to murder her, Mr. Queen? If freedom and security were my client's objectives, as you say, I'd hardly recommend his method as a means of getting them."

"Nor would I, Mr. Irons." said Ellery, "but let's not anticipate. Your client is full of surprises. May I go on, before that jury comes in?"

And Ellery continued even more rapidly: "A year or so ago Dirk Lawrence began to evince an abnormal jealousy–it was an obsession, almost a phobia. Let's integrate it. Since nothing in this case so far has turned out what it seemed–since the deceived husband was in reality the scheming killer–we must question everything he did. Was his jealousy genuine, or was it not? The answer must be that it was not, for a man suffering from a genuine complex of jealousy would hardly conspire to entangle his wife in an affair with another man!

"The jealousy attacks were faked.

"But if we regard Lawrence's jealousy attacks as faked, then his whole plan spreads before us in all its naked ugliness.

"He would pretend to be a jealous husband, establishing himself as ridden by morbid fears of his wife's 'infidelity.' He would carefully develop this pretense over a great many months, creating an atmosphere of suspicion and inducing an attitude of acceptance on the part of his and his wife's friends–with particular attention to Miss Porter and myself. Then he would unleash his accomplice to drag Martha into the appearance of a clandestine affair. This would be built up, by the accomplice at Lawrence's direction, with the romantic trappings of the classic adultery– a 'code,' a book as the code-key, secret meetings all over town, with occasional 'lapses' of discretion on the part of the 'lover' so that they could be seen in public; and so on. Finally, the poor obsessed husband would be vindicated. He would actually overhear a telephone conversation naming an immediate rendezvous at the other man's house. He would rush out in pursuit. He would surprise his wife and the other man in the other man's bedroom … and, snatching up the other man's gun in the shock and frenzy of the 'discovery,' he would kill them both–before witnesses, for he knew that Harrison's man was there, and he knew that Nikki Porter was a spy in his own household and that I was in the case nose-down, hot on his trail.

"Yes, Mr. Irons, your client figured out a way to commit murder for profit and live to have his profit, too. For what has your defense been? Lawrence's defense? The unwritten law, Mr. Irons–the law that's not on the statute books but has nevertheless freed every defendant who was ever able to plead it under the facts!

"You, I, Judge Levy, the State's Attorney here–and Dirk Lawrence–all know that the tradition of the unwritten law in this country and all over the Western world has been to free the wronged victim of the adultery. Juries just don't convict husbands of murder who have caught their wives in adulterous relationships with other men before witnesses–as you so rightly pointed out to this jury, Mr. Irons. Your very real confidence as to the outcome of this case–up to a few minutes ago–is eloquent testimony to that fact. It's a confidence, I'm sure, your client shares at this moment.

"Oh, yes, Dirk Lawrence was taking a chance. It was a gamble. But a very good gamble. His own father had committed the same kind of murder and had been found not guilty!–undoubtedly the source of Dirk's inspiration. The record was all in his favor, and if it was a gamble, look at the stakes he was gambling for. A fortune of millions. Many a man has run the risk of the electric chair or scaffold or gas chamber for a great deal less."

And at this moment the court attendant knocked on Judge Levy's door, and he said, "Excuse me, Your Honor. The jury's reached a verdict. They're getting ready to come out."

"Don't open that door again," thundered the judge, "until I call you!"

The State's Attorney got up, sat down. He lit a cigaret nervously.

Darrell Irons got up, but he did not sit down again. He went to the window to look out at Bridgeport, the fireless cigar clenched in his teeth.

"Too late." Ellery was saying. "Too damn late! It's a not-guilty finding, of course. They couldn't reach any other decision on the basis of the evidence presented to them. Congratulations, Mr. Irons! Once that jury gives its verdict, Lawrence can thumb his nose at the pack of us and the universe thrown in. Under the rule of double jeopardy, he'll have got away with premeditated, cold-blooded murder!"

"No," said Irons, without turning.

"No," said Judge Levy. "Not yet, Mr. Queen. Under the law, regardless of what the jury has decided in the jury room, there is no verdict until the presiding judge instructs the clerk of the court to ask the jury for it. This case isn't closed by a long shot. And it won't be closed until after I take my place on the bench out there."

"But I thought—"

"Never mind what you thought, Mr. Queen. I want that proof you promised. The evidence you said would be acceptable to the court."

Ellery inhaled. "Yes, sir! I've had only a few hours to dig, but even in that short time I was able to unearth two heretofore unproduced facts which support my theory and lift it from speculation to the realm of evidence.

"The first is legally not so important as the second, but it proves my original thesis that Martha Lawrence was not in love with Van Harrison and that her affair with Harrison was a frame-up engineered by the defendant.

"At my request, the prosecutor sent out one of the exhibits in the case to a laboratory for analysis. The exhibit, you'll recall, was the bundle of love letters found in Harrison's bedroom desk and presumed to have been written by Martha to Harrison. The analysis I requested the lab to make was an ink analysis.

"The reason I requested an ink analysis of the letters was that some odd facts had struck me. There were no envelopes to any of the letters, and none bore a date—only days of the week were named. Also, none of the salutations specifically named *Harrison;* the letters merely began, 'My dearest,' 'Darling,' and so on. In other words, from the letters themselves, there was no evidence that they dated from Martha's friendship with Harrison, or that they had been written to Harrison. He was presumed to have been the addressee because the letters were found on his premises.

"I phoned the laboratory just before I stepped into this room.

"Their report was that the ink on those letters is at least four, probably five, years old.

"Martha Lawrence met Van Harrison for the first time no earlier than a few months ago. This was brought out during the trial. It can undoubtedly be further corroborated.

"*Therefore Mrs. Lawrence could not possibly have written those letters to Van Harrison*. How, then, did they get into the drawer of Harrison's bedroom desk? And even more important, why were they there at all? These are inescapable questions.

"Were they there for blackmail purposes? But passionate letters from a married woman to a lover have no value for blackmail purposes unless they bear dates, name names, and can be connected incontrovertibly with the individual involved. The publication of those letters as they stand would not connect them with Van Harrison—or with any other man exclusively—and any threat to publish them would therefore be an empty one.

"But if they didn't serve a blackmail purpose for Harrison, what purpose could they have served? A sentimental one? They were not even written to him.

"The more you puzzle over these letters," said Ellery, "the clearer it becomes that the only purpose they were meant to serve was the purpose they did serve—that is, to be found, to be presumed to have been written to Harrison, to furnish additional documentation to the appearance of an ordinary illicit affair between Harrison and Martha Lawrence.

"There is confirmation of this. When I visited Harrison's house that night to warn him away from Martha, a very convenient telephone call took him out of the house for half an hour or so, leaving me on the premises alone, as I testified. On analysis, if Harrison had been conducting a genuine amour with a woman married to a jealous husband, the last thing in the world he would have done was to leave an interested party on the premises—a known investigator—giving him a clear field to search for and find such 'damaging' evidence of the affair! Knowing I was coming, Harrison had evidently ordered Martha to phone him, so that he would have an excuse for leaving the house that would in turn allow me to find the evidence I subsequently testified to in court.

"Then where did Harrison get those letters? They could only have come from the man to whom they had been originally written. Martha Lawrence—and this can be proved in court—had only one love affair prior to her meeting with Harrison and within the past four or five years—the age of the ink—and that was with her husband. She told me herself she had written many love letters to Dirk during their courtship. If the facts can be established to the satisfaction of the Court—and I believe they can—then the conclusion is plain: The letters found in Harrison's possession came from Dirk Lawrence—*Dirk Lawrence gave them to Harrison.* The presumption must be that Lawrence did so for the express purpose that they subsequently served, since there is no other reasonable explanation. Lawrence destroyed the telltale envelopes, and he made a careful selection of those letters only in which no date appeared, no name in the salutation, and no reference in the text which would give the show away.

"The provable facts about the letters, then, with the reasonable presumptions arising from them, confirm my theory that Martha Lawrence was framed by Dirk Lawrence.

"The second thing I was able to dig out today," Ellery went on, hardly pausing for breath, "is damning, and on its weight alone I would rest my case.

"It was brought out during the trial that Van Harrison's substantial deposits in his savings accounts coincided perfectly with Martha Lawrence's withdrawals from her accounts. But until today no one—and I don't except myself—thought of checking *Harrison's withdrawals.*

"First let me expand my theory a bit. I had postulated a deal between Lawrence and Harrison, under the terms of which Harrison was to embroil Lawrence's wife in the appearance of an adulterous relationship. While the novelty of this situation must have appealed to Harrison's sardonic make-up, he would hardly have entered into such an agreement purely for the sake of its novelty. It was dangerous, illegal, and if it ever came out he would find himself behind bars. To run such a risk, Harrison could only have been tempted by the prospect of money, a great deal of money. Lawrence, then, must have offered him a considerable monetary inducement.

"Lawrence also had to offer Harrison a plausible reason to explain his own position in the deal. Harrison was no fool; and even if he were, he'd have to have been an absolute idiot not to question Lawrence's motives before agreeing to such an unusual proposal.

"What sort of motive could Lawrence have dreamed up to explain why he was doing this? The simplest possible, the one most likely to convince Harrison–in fact, Lawrence's real motive, if in abbreviated and twisted form. That is, Lawrence must have told Harrison that he, too, was in it for the money he could get out of it. He must have proved to Harrison that Martha's fortune was all in her name, he must have said that she refused to give him any substantial part of it, that he needed money desperately, and that the only way he could get any of it was to blackmail her through a third party. Harrison was to blackmail Martha Lawrence through a means which Lawrence would put in Harrison's hand, and Harrison and Lawrence would split what Harrison got out of her.

"I arrived, then, at a theoretical conclusion that Harrison had been paying some of the blackmail money he got from Martha Lawrence over to Dirk Lawrence. A kick-back. A rake-off. Could I prove it?

"I proved it, gentlemen," said Ellery grimly, "by checking Harrison's withdrawals from his various accounts. I went over those accounts and made notes of his withdrawals. I saw that each time Harrison deposited a substantial sum, *he withdrew within a day or so exactly half of that deposit.*

"I then went to Dirk Lawrence's bank and checked Lawrence's deposits. They show that, within a day or so of Van Harrison's withdrawals, *Dirk Lawrence deposited the identical sums in his personal account.*

"The identical nature and synchronization of Harrison's withdrawals and Lawrence's deposits can't possibly be dismissed as coincidences. There are too many of them–the same amounts, on dates consistently within a day or so of each other.

"If that doesn't prove to the satisfaction of this or any other court and jury that Lawrence and Harrison were confederates; that Lawrence was not the innocent husband in an ordinary case of adultery; that he was a secret, third party to the affair, unknown to the wife; that therefore his shooting of Harrison and Martha Lawrence was done not to avenge his honor but to shut Harrison's mouth and gain Martha's fortune—if that doesn't prove it, gentlemen, I'll make a public apology to Dirk Lawrence in that courtroom and take an oath never to stick my nose into another case.

"Here are my notes on Harrison's withdrawals; the original bank records from which they come are on exhibit in the courtroom. Here are my notes on Lawrence's matching deposits; they come from the records of the Equity Savings Bank of New York, Fifth Avenue branch, where I got them this afternoon."

The judge, the prosecutor, and the defense attorney bent over the papers Ellery had laid on the desk.

Five minutes later, the judge and the prosecutor resumed their seats in silence, and in silence Darrell Irons went back to his window.

Ellery waited.

He was painfully conscious that the jury was waiting, too, beyond the judge's door.

And Dirk …

"There are some features of this case I still don't comprehend," murmured Judge Levy at last. "I understand how Lawrence could talk Harrison into collaborating on a blackmail plot, but what reason did he give Harrison for simultaneously making it look like an adultery case? Lawrence could scarcely tell Harrison that the adultery was necessary so that he, Lawrence, could murder his wife—and Harrison! — and get off on the plea of the unwritten law. Yet he must have given Harrison some reason that Harrison found plausible. What is the answer to that, Mr. Queen?"

Ellery shrugged. "Lawrence's obvious line was to tell Harrison that his ultimate goal was a divorce. They would milk Martha out of as much as they could through blackmail, and meanwhile Harrison would be laying the groundwork for a future divorce action to be brought by Lawrence on the charge of adultery, with Harrison the co-respondent.

"This completely explains Harrison's cooperation … the trail he deliberately laid for me at Lawrence's instructions or even direction—because undoubtedly Lawrence knew from the beginning what Miss Porter and I were about, and used us very cleverly to further his greater scheme, just as he used Harrison. And Harrison made a very good job of it. He nominated as the very first rendezvous a hotel room. He em-

163

braced and kissed Martha whenever he knew or suspected I was watching. He brought her to his home and made her go up to his bedroom with him repeatedly, so that his houseman might later be able to testify to the fact—although Harrison hardly foresaw that Tama would testify to the fact at a murder trial in which he himself was the murderee! He willingly planted some of Martha's personal effects—clothing which of course Dirk Lawrence provided—in one of his bedroom closets, to be found by me and any other party interested in getting evidence for a divorce action. Harrison even went so far as to tell me, in so many words, that he was sleeping with Martha Lawrence. It was a lie, of course, since he could only have been an object of horror to her, but a lie he quite cheerfully told in laying the groundwork for Lawrence of what Harrison never doubted would be a divorce action … Yes, Van Harrison was Dirk Lawrence's willing dupe; and the great irony is that after manipulating his puppets with skill and bringing his plot cleverly and successfully up to its climax, Lawrence flubbed it. His aim wavered, and he failed to kill Martha. He'd done it all for nothing."

The men were silent.

Then Judge Levy said, "I'm still puzzled, Mr. Queen. After all, Mrs. Lawrence did go to a hotel with that man, she did visit his home and repeatedly retire to his bedroom with him, she did suffer him to embrace her in public, and so forth. How did Harrison make Mrs. Lawrence acquiesce to this appearance of an affair? What was the nature of the weapon Lawrence put into Harrison's hand that compelled Mrs. Lawrence's obedience to his orders?"

Ellery shrugged. "Dirk Lawrence was the only man Martha ever loved. As often happens to a woman who finds her only love relatively late—she was over thirty when she met and married Lawrence—it was for her the epic passion. Whatever the weapon was, then, it was probably aimed at her love for Lawrence. The weapon must have implicated Lawrence in some very serious way, must have seemed to aim an extreme threat to him.

"The most extreme threat, of course, would have been a threat against Lawrence's life. Suppose Martha thought that by playing Harrison's game *she was saving her beloved's life?*"

"A crime he'd committed!" said the judge.

"The extreme crime," nodded Ellery. "Why not? Murder. But not necessarily a murder he had *committed*, Your Honor. All that was required was for Martha to *believe* he had committed a murder. This man is capable of anything, even of concocting a phony murder rap against himself!—an easily exposed phony, of course, so that his safety couldn't be threatened by, say, Harrison's suddenly turning against him; but a phony convincing enough to pull the wool over the eyes of the woman who loved him.

"I think Lawrence gave Harrison some false document or other, prepared by himself, which seemed to prove that Lawrence had murdered someone, and I think Harrison showed this document to Martha and told her that unless she paid him blackmail he would turn it over to the police and send her precious husband to the chair. Something Martha once told me and Miss Porter bolsters this theory. Not long before they met, while Lawrence worked for a publishing house, he became intimate with a girl who was also employed there. The girl, Martha told us, committed suicide.

"Lawrence might well have adapted this incident from his past to the needs of his plan. He might have manufactured evidence to indicate, not that the girl committed suicide, but that to get rid of her he had murdered her.

"And Martha—poor Martha—didn't dare let on even to Lawrence ... especially to Lawrence! ... what she was mixed up in, for fear of some 'reckless' action on his part which might bring the whole thing out in the open and seal his fate. And, very likely, the clever Mr. Lawrence—whose ability to concoct fictional murder plots is now brought into revealing focus—undoubtedly got that document back after it had served its vicious purpose. He'd hardly have permitted Harrison to hold on to it, to be found in Harrison's effects after the shooting. So unless Lawrence confesses this part of it, or Martha survives to tell her story, the exact nature of the blackmail weapon Lawrence manufactured for Harrison's use may never be established."

"But what reason did Harrison give Mrs. Lawrence," asked the judge, "for these adulterous-looking assignations? It seems to me she'd have suspected a frame-up from Harrison's conduct."

"I doubt it. Harrison had the best blind in the world for his behavior. He was known as a great lover. It would not have seemed so strange to

Martha that, in addition to making her pay him blackmail, Harrison should also try to make time with her. She was probably too busy fighting him off to probe too deeply into his real motive. It would not surprise me, in fact, if Harrison developed a genuine interest in the chase; the situation would have appealed to his cynical make-up. Or, for that matter, if Dirk Lawrence knew it."

And Ellery stopped thoughtfully.

And then he said, "And I think, Your Honor, that's all of it."

Darrell Irons turned from the window.

"Judge Levy." he said, "I wish it explicitly understood that I agreed to defend this case in good faith and because I believed in the validity of my client's injury. I don't any longer hold to that belief. I withdraw from the defense."

And at a later time the members of another jury filed back into the courtroom from the jury room, and they took their seats, and a man at a table gripped the arms of his chair and looked from face to face in the jury box as if he were trying to discover a well-kept secret; and another judge nodded to the clerk of the court; and the courtroom was still.

And the clerk of the court turned to face the jury box, and he said in a clear voice: "Will the foreman of the jury please rise?"

And a man in the first seat of the first row of the jury box rose.

And the clerk of the court said: "Has the jury arrived at a verdict?"

And the foreman of the jury replied: "We have."

And the clerk asked: "How does the jury find?"

And the foreman of the jury turned to look Dirk Lawrence full in the face, and he said with considerable distinctness: "We find the defendant guilty of murder in the first degree."

And in a little room adjoining the courtroom a pale woman rose and said with a sigh to the man and the girl beside her, "Please take me home."

Lightning Source UK Ltd.
Milton Keynes UK
UKOW03f0700260314

228841UK00001B/30/P